HEIST
DURING THE
RIO GAMES

HEIST
DURING THE
RIO GAMES

DEXTER JAMES

iUniverse®

HEIST DURING THE RIO GAMES

iUniverse books may be ordered through booksellers or by contacting:

iUniverse
1663 Liberty Drive
Bloomington, IN 47403
www.iuniverse.com
1-800-Authors (1-800-288-4677)

Because of the dynamic nature of the Internet, any web addresses or links contained in this book may have changed since publication and may no longer be valid. The views expressed in this work are solely those of the author and do not necessarily reflect the views of the publisher, and the publisher hereby disclaims any responsibility for them.

Any people depicted in stock imagery provided by Thinkstock are models, and such images are being used for illustrative purposes only. Certain stock imagery © Thinkstock.

ISBN: 978-1-4917-9669-6 (sc)
ISBN: 978-1-4917-9668-9 (e)

Library of Congress Control Number: 2016907196

Print information available on the last page.

iUniverse rev. date: 04/29/2016

OTHER BOOKS BY DEXTER JAMES:

Genesis Déjà vu – The Beginning

To my granddaughters

Gracie, Abbie, Jane, Chloe and Nora

Contents

PART 3 – THE STING

Acknowledgements

Special thanks to both Terry Connolly and Diane Richardson for taking the time to read through the manuscript and offering their feedback. I know both of them have much better things to do with their time which is why their suggestions are all the more appreciated.

As a result, any errors in the book are all of my own doing and I trust they do not detract from what I hope is an enjoyable read.

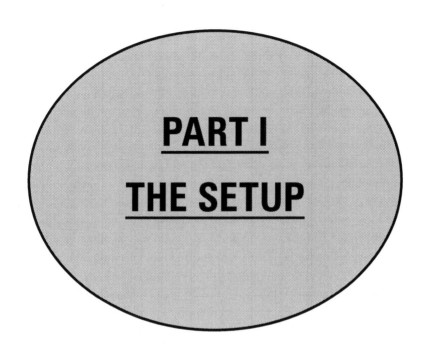

PART I

THE SETUP

CHAPTER 1

The Prison

The Rotunda was a male-only, state-of-the-art, top security prison built to incarcerate high-risk criminals and terrorists. When it was first announced that the establishment would be built in a former logging community in Northern Ontario, the local inhabitants were vehemently opposed to the proposal. However, after realizing the number of jobs it would create and the service industry that would be generated as a result of the institution, the attitude of the mostly unemployed adults living in the area quickly changed.

The remoteness of the institution was another reason why this particular location was chosen. The nearest airport was over fifty kilometers away and that was merely a municipal one, catering mainly to floatplanes taking fisherman to remote camps for a long week-end. The railway line that had once brought supplies to a thriving community had not been maintained since the demise of the area's logging trade. Only one main road provided any communication with the area and the outside world. The authorities thought process was that no prison escapees would have any access to transportation and even if they did, their paths for escape were severely limited. For five kilometers surrounding the facility there was just swamp land with nowhere to hide. The only entrance to the prison was via the exit off the main highway onto the single road leading to the institution's heavily guarded gates and the car park, situated just inside the gates. The car park was for prisoners' visitors, guards, and support staff. There was a building housing a comfortable waiting room and facilities where the staff and guests could wait in between shuttle buses that would take them to the main building. The whole stretch of the five kilometer long road, named the Rotunda Expressway, was clearly visible from the twin towers that straddled either side of the prison's gate. The tower guards had direct communication with the command center located inside the Rotunda and personnel in either location were able to close the exit barriers to and from the main highway in the unlikely event an escapee made it that far. Within the establishment, guards could raise any of the four remotely deployable spike strips built in to the road, positioned at one kilometer intervals along the Rotunda Expressway. Anti-crash barriers along the length of the road prevented any hope of evading the machines once their protruding prongs were primed.

Around the square perimeter of the Rotunda was a six meter high, thick, wire mesh fence topped with razor wire. At the corners of the perimeter were towers containing armed guards and on the sides and back of the perimeter, positioned halfway along their lengths were additional towers. The nine towers provide an unobstructed view of the open ground between the Rotunda, the inner fence, and all nine were in direct communication with each other and the command center. Inside that was the inner fence which was a five meter high electric fence, again capped with razor wire that surrounded the exercise areas and playing fields around the actual building called the Rotunda. The Rotunda itself was a white, three-tiered circular structure which the locals affectionately called the 'wedding cake'. The bottom tier consisted of thick reinforced concrete and housed the cells that encompassed the outside of the building with strategically placed gaps for access to the workout fields and the main entrance. With the exception of the main entrance, the gaps were accessed through double doors controlled by the command center. The main entrance at the end of the Rotunda Expressway was flanked by two guard houses and they controlled the sliding metal doors that protected the entrance to the Rotunda. One guard house was situated on the inside of the door, the other on the outside. Before the door could be opened the guards contacted one another and both had to activate a switch before the doors would open.

Each cell had accommodation for one prisoner and was made of a thick polymer insert that nestled neatly into specially designed niches in the concrete wall. The insert included a clear, thick, glass window that provided some natural light for the inmate. The opening and closing of the cell doors were controlled by the command center. For each prisoner there were set times for showers and meals but in between these set times there were few restrictions to the number of activities in which a prisoner could participate. The prisoner merely made a request by accessing an intercom embedded in the wall of the cell. His intentions were made known to the guards patrolling the inside perimeter of the cells and they escorted the prisoner to his destination. This was possible because as far as correctional facilities go, the Rotunda had a very high ratio of officers to prisoners. Beyond the cells, at frequent intervals, were shower blocks and further towards the center was the dining area. The outer area of the next level provided games rooms, gymnasiums and the prison library. These facilities were accessed by either stairs or elevators for those prisoners with medical conditions. The inner area of this level housed the guards, administration offices and medical center. The guards were on eight hour shifts and when on duty spent two hours walking the inside perimeter of the cells, two hours general duties, dining area, shower supervision etc. and two hours in the emergency pool, to be called upon as and if necessary. That left them two hours for meal and administration breaks. In addition, a rotation was scheduled by the warden to cover the towers, gates and prison complex. The warden felt that constantly changing duties would help alleviate complacency and keep the guards sharp. The division of the outer and inner areas were serviced by cutover doors that provided access for the guards and for the transportation of the prisoners. These cutover doors were operated by the command center which was situated on the top level of the building.

The command center was a technological marvel with video surveillance covering the entire complex, capable of observing every access into and out of the fences, building and cells. It also had automated controls for emergency procedures, lockdowns, broadcasting canned messages across the speaker system and sending alarms to other emergency services and military units. Each inmate wore a wrist bracelet with a unique bar code that could be read by sensors detailing his whereabouts at any given time. These wristbands required special tools to safely remove them without sending alarms to the command center. During emergencies or lockdowns a head count was automatically issued and alarms were immediately raised if the wristband count was not correctly reconciled with the number of current inmates. Furthermore, the wristbands were detected at checkpoints in and out of the buildings as well as the entrance gates. Any escaping prisoner would have to somehow remove the wristband with the appropriate tool to avoid raising the attention of the guards at these checkpoints.

In the event of a power failure backup generators automatically kicked in and there were even backup generators for the backups. Even if they failed, all the cells and access points would automatically be in lock-down mode and would only be able to be opened by special keys kept in the command center. It would come as no surprise to anyone to learn there had been no successful breakouts from this prison, however; that was about to change.

CHAPTER 2

Role Reversal

It was on this particular day, just after 2:00 PM on a typically cold, bleak, fall afternoon. The prison guards were changing shift. The majority of them were in the emergency pool room exchanging friendly banter. Those who were just finishing their shift were preparing to leave on the shuttle bus to the main entrance and the prison car park. The guards on the new shift were reviewing their day's assignments. It was a Tuesday and the warden was in the building for the regular weekly meeting with his three shift commanders. Lunch had finished and most of the prisoners were relaxing in their cells; a few were in the games room and gym with one inmate studying in the library. The number of guards required to accompany the inmates was allocated depending on the location of the inmates and the risk status of the prisoners in a given location. On this day, only a skeleton guard escort was deemed necessary and the usual guard complement was supervising the perimeter. Brian Beasley was in the library, where he spent most of his recreational time. Brian was tall, slim and athletic but because his behavior had been exemplary since coming to the establishment it was felt only one guard was necessary to accompany him. That guard was sitting in an armchair, firmly entrenched in a copy of the day's sports pages.

The library housed only a few books, daily papers, and magazines; however, the prison had an arrangement with one of the national book chains that allowed inmates to download, via the internet, any book in stock onto a reading tablet. Each prisoner was given a tablet on his arrival at the establishment and given instructions on how to use it. Brian had just finished downloading a latest bestseller when he noticed the jovial exchange between the guards had ceased and they were hastily donning bulletproof vests and riot gear. Above him he could see personnel in the command center making frantic efforts to communicate with others on landline phones, cell phones and two-way radios. The other strange thing was that the library door he was standing next to had unexpectedly slid open as had the cutover door nearest to the library, but strangely, the doorways to the administration buildings were all locked down, as were those of the games room and gym.

Because Brian just happened to be standing by the library door. He nonchalantly stepped through the open doorway seconds before the door suddenly slid shut behind him. This caught the attention of his guard who looked up from the paper he was reading in reaction to the unexpected opening of the door. But he was too late. The guard was now imprisoned in the library while his charge was walking freely outside.

Brian was aware that when a lockdown occurs, alarms and speakers are activated, but for some strange reason this appeared to be a silent lockdown. Or was it so strange? Brian thought. He stood there for a few seconds, casually, in full view of the trapped guards in the command center, listening and looking for any guards not in the command center that may be responding to the lockdown. But incredibly, all the guards appeared to be locked up. It appeared that the inmates had taken over the asylum, or in this case, just the one inmate.

Brian slowly walked forward through the cutover door and as he did so he noticed that some of the guards in the command center were pointing guns at him in threatening gestures, others were trying to open the locked command center doors with their manual override keys but inconceivably, they were not working. Brian knew that gesticulating with their guns was just for show as firing their guns would have been a dangerous proposition. The walls of the buildings were bullet proof and ricochets could cause injury or even a fatality in the command center itself. With this in mind he continued to walk around the circular office structure with total indifference. In the middle of the commotion he could see the warden barking out orders at the operators feverishly flicking switches and pushing buttons in an effort to bring some semblance of order to the growing chaos. Brian merely smiled and continued strolling towards the service area at the front of the building. No service deliveries were allowed an hour either side of shift changes for security reasons, so the only vehicles at the entrance was the guards' shuttle bus and the warden's black sedan with the tinted windows. Down below, on the prisoners' level he could see the perimeter guards patrolling the cells, unaware that silent pandemonium was breaking out above them. Brian decided to carry on walking.

In the command center all security cameras had blacked out, their land-line phones, which are serviced by the internet, were dead and their cell phones were displaying no signals. Every channel of their two-way radios appeared to be jammed and the computer was not responding to their attempts to reverse the lockdown or open any of the doors.

Brian continued to walk nonchalantly through the service area and headed for the warden's car. He opened the unlocked door on the driver's side and got in. The keys were still in the ignition and on the passenger seat was the warden's cap with its gold braid on the peak. Brian calmly undid his prison overalls and pulled them off his torso to reveal a white shirt. He ripped off the back of his reading tablet and inside was a piece of tin foil placed there by the manufacturer to provide protection to the circuit board. Brian carefully tore out the foil and wrapped it three times round the bar code of his security wristband then made sure the cuffs of his shirt concealed the foil. He was a little disappointed his tablet was now ruined as he hadn't got to read the last book he had downloaded in the library which was entitled 'The Great Escape'.

He placed the warden's cap on his head, adjusted it and took a look in the rear-view mirror to ensure the hat was correctly positioned. Brian then started the car and proceeded to drive through the tunnel to the Rotunda's entrance. As he approached the guardhouse on the inside of the tunnel entrance the guards recognized the vehicle and started the procedures for opening the door. These guards had no reason to suspect there was a problem in the Rotunda, nor that the very doors to their own guardhouses were locked. Their security cameras, like those of the tower guards were unaffected by the blackout as their views were restricted to their immediate vicinities, not the entire complex.

It was not unusual to see the warden's car at this time on a Tuesday, consequently, Brian just drove past the guards with neither of them any the wiser that it was an escapee driving the car. The tin foil around Brian's wristband reflected any signals issued from the sensors and he continued to drive to the gates of the facility. The guards on the outside perimeter recognized the warden's car and the gates were already open as Brian approached. He offered a quick wave as he drove through the gates and he was on his way to the highway.

Brian kept to the speed limit to avoid any unwanted suspicion and soon made it to the main road. Before he knew it he was on the highway past the local town and into the country. After a while he looked into his rear view mirror and noticed what appeared to be an unmarked police cruiser very close behind him. Ahead of him was an exit that indicated it was a historical site for an old logging camp. Brian indicated and took the exit; the other car continued to follow him. Brian then saw a small disused logging road and he slowed down and turned into it. He drove another kilometer until he was faced with some timbers and old heavy-duty logging machinery blocking the road. As he stopped he noticed that the car that had been following him had pulled up behind him. Brian watched as the driver's door slowly opened and a beautiful young woman exited the car. Brian took off the warden's cap and got out of his car and said to the woman, "I'm afraid I have taken a wrong turning." The woman just smiled and replied, "why don't you ride with me? Perhaps I can help you get to where you want to go?" Then Brian walked towards her and she passed him a pair of wire cutters. Brian used them to cut through the security wristband. He placed the remnants of the wristband into the warden's cap and tossed the whole thing onto the front seat of the warden's car.

Barely ten minutes later, dressed in an immaculate, expensive suit, Brian and his lady friend were on their way to the Toronto airport with the warden's car safely hidden in the undergrowth where it wouldn't be found for another few days by a couple of local, curious, young teenagers.

"So everything went to plan Brian?" The lady asked.

"Without a hitch," Brian replied.

"How long do we have before an all-points bulletin is issued?" The lady inquired.

"The first ones to respond to the problem will be the tower guards." Brian said with confidence. "Their doors are not controlled by the command center but the guards are conditioned not to leave their post under any circumstance, unless relieved. As their reliefs are all locked up it will be a couple of hours before one of them summons up the courage to climb down the tower and drive to the main building. After finding out everyone is locked up and the phones aren't working they will have to drive to the town to alert the authorities and contact technical support to fix the computer glitch. Which means they will have to walk back to the prison gates, because the spike strips would have been activated by then. Once they are at the prison gates they will have difficulty opening them but eventually I'm sure an ingenious guard will manage it somehow. Then and only then one of the guards will be able to get into a vehicle to drive into town to report the problem."

"So the police could be looking for us in a couple of hours." The lady stated, quite concerned.

"Whoops, forgot to mention, the barriers to and from the highway have shut down; the only way to alert the authorities is by walking into town. Furthermore, the tower guards are not even aware that anyone has escaped. I estimate, at the very earliest, at least twelve hours. By then we are on the plane and out of the country."

"Why can't they use cell phones?" The lady asked.

"Simple." Brian replied as if it was obvious. "Before the Rotunda was built the area had no cell access. In their wisdom, the telephone companies thought it would be more secure from vandals if they built the new cell tower in the grounds of the prison. So, even when the town folk notify the telephone company that they don't have signals, technicians won't be able to fix it remotely and it will be a while before they are able to get on-site access."

"So you have thought of everything." The lady said impressed.

"We'll soon find out." Brian replied, secretly knowing that yes, he had thought of everything, he had spent the best part of a year planning it.

"What I don't understand," the lady mused, "is why nobody questioned why you would even be sent to this establishment."

"Maybe it was how much I had embezzled, who it was from and the fact that the money has never been recovered." Brian said.

"Even so," the lady replied, "locking you up in a facility that is controlled entirely by computers just doesn't make sense. Someone there must have known you were convicted of embezzlement and that you hacked into computers to do it."

CHAPTER 3

A Trip South

Within a few hours of his escape Brian and his lady friend were approaching the car rental terminal at Toronto Pearson International Airport. In terms of driving distance the prison was just about equidistant between the Toronto and Detroit international airports. They had planned to fly to Rio de Janeiro and would have preferred to cross to the U.S. at the Windsor/Detroit border. But unfortunately, there were no direct flights to Rio from Detroit, but there were from Toronto. In fact, most of the travel web sites showed connections at Toronto from Detroit to Rio which would have defeated the objective of attempting to leave the country as soon as possible. So, they settled on booking a flight from Toronto which departed later in the evening. Their reasoning was that by the time the authorities had got their searches and road blocks in position they would at least be through the departure gates and would be an innocuous looking couple waiting for a flight that had been booked for almost a month.

Brian's lady friend had already printed their boarding passes on-line so they approached the security gate with their carry-on luggage. The officer visually scanned the passports of Peter Pasque and Sandra Essex and reconciled them with their boarding passes. Peter's Canadian passport correctly described him as 5ft. 11 ins. tall with brown eyes and dark hair. What it didn't tell the female officer was that he was slim, athletic and extremely handsome. She could see that all too obviously for herself. She quickly glanced at the man posing as Peter before turning to his lady friend, Sandra. Her passport indicated Sandra Essex, 5ft. 6 ins. tall, with blue eyes and blonde hair but the officer was less concerned with her beauty and with a slight sense of envy she returned the passports to the two travelers.

Brian and Sandra extracted their laptop computers and tablets from their one small carry-on bag that they each had and placed everything on the conveyor belt for security inspection. Once through security they headed for the V.I.P. lounge, produced their boarding passes clearly proving they were occupants of first class seating and found a remote table in the executive lounge and relaxed. Up until this point, with all the adrenalin running on a high of excitement, Brian suddenly realized how hungry he was. The fact was neither of them had eaten since lunch time and it was now late evening. They found a seat and immediately began to fill a plate full of sandwiches and salads. At about the same time they were enjoying their second drink and plate of food, back at the Rotunda one of the guards at the prison had dared to leave his tower.

By the time Brian and Sandra were in the air and settling down to sleep, back in Ontario, the first emergency calls were being received by the authorities. The authorities were conducting a full search in Ontario just as Brian and Sandra's passports were being scanned, by customs and immigration in Brazil. Needless to say, their passports were fake, Peter and Sandra were not their real names and the officer was sliding the bar codes printed on the passports through an OCR machine. Brian was watching the officer and he appeared satisfied with the details on his computer screen, consequently, it was with great relief when Brian and Gracie, which was Sandra's real name, accepted their passports back from the officer. They had survived this test, the one they considered the weakest link in the plan. To say they both had butterflies in their stomachs would have been a gross understatement but they fully managed to display a bright exuberant exterior typical of a couple traveling on their honeymoon, which is exactly what they told the officer in their combination of poor Portuguese and English.

They were quickly through into the main terminal and were expecting to be picked up by a local couple who would take them to an apartment Gracie had discovered during a previous trip to Rio. As they faced the throng of people awaiting passengers from the various incoming flights Gracie scanned the faces to locate the couple she had met on her previous trip. Sure enough, much to Gracie's relief, there in the front row behind the barrier was the young lady, accompanied by the man. The man was holding a sign high in the air which said, in English, 'WELCOME PETER AND SANDRA'. Gracie led Brian over to the couple and introduced them. The man's name was Cristiano and her name was Celia, hugs and greetings were exchanged then they left the airport in a beat up old Fiat. The apartment Gracie had rented was in Copacabana and this was where they were headed. In the afternoon traffic Cristiano informed them it would take approximately an hour before they arrived at their destination. The plan was for Brian and Gracie to stay there for a while until all the excitement had died down, then they could began planning for their future. After all, Brian and Gracie were getting married tomorrow, which is why they could say with all honesty to the immigration officer that they were here for their honeymoon, except they were not getting married to each other.

CHAPTER 4

Getting Married

Brian knew that, except for a very few isolated cases, Brazil is famous for not extraditing their citizens to any country. He also knew that it was possible to obtain Brazilian citizenship within one year of marrying a natural born Brazilian. Brian anticipated that the whole legal procedure of extraditing him from Brazil back to Canada would take much longer than a year. But there was another risk; the extradition restrictions applied only to natural born Brazilian citizens. So there was a small chance that even if Brian obtained his Brazilian citizenship he could still be extradited. Although it was extremely unlikely that the Brazilian authorities would uphold the extradition order for someone who embezzled a great deal of money from a lot of rich bankers without using any violence whatsoever. Especially if he was prepared to invest all of those ill-gotten gains in his new country of residence.

So it was that in a double ceremony in a Civil Registry office in the district of Copacabana Brian Beasley was married to Celia Ronaldo. To be a own was married to Cristiano Aguera. The trip Gracie had made to Rio a couple of months ago during the apartment search was also to find a couple who would be prepared to marry for a generous amount of money. Once that was achieved, all the necessary paperwork for the marriages would have to be arranged, which was carried out with Celia's assistance. Brian's absence was easily explained away with a small bribe and a double flash of Gracie and Celia's ample breasts.

After the ceremony the two couples, now back with their regular partners retired to a small bistro to celebrate. The terms that had been discussed for the arrangement with Cristiano and Celia were settled in cash and Brian also paid for the celebration. They parted company in the knowledge that there was no need to contact each other again until the ultimate divorce proceedings became necessary. But that was not expected for at least a year and a few months.

Brian placed ads. for the obligatory marriage announcements in the local newspapers and they were to be published the next day. Then Brian went online to the major Toronto newspapers and placed the very same announcements there. He was certain that some representative in the Royal Canadian Mounted Police would pick up on it but to be sure he sent an email, using an untraceable email account, to his arresting police officer, Detective Superintendent Dexter Davis, to look out for the announcement. This would at least call off the hounds looking for him back home. He felt that was the least he could do.

Other than that, no further notifications were necessary. Gracie was an orphan so as far as parents and siblings were concerned there would be no surprises for anyone. Possibly a few friends would get to hear of the marriage but she really didn't care about them. As for Brian, he had alienated his parents a long time ago. They had more or less disowned him during his early crime spree days. They tried to direct him back on the straight and narrow with therapists and hospital sessions but to no avail. So the embezzlement conviction was as much as they could take: they sold their home and moved to the west coast. Brian no longer knew their address or how to contact them and was certain they wouldn't care about his nuptial celebrations, even if they were to be made aware of them. Although, he could thank them for the entry level position he took at the bank. Brian's father, in a last ditch effort, persuaded one of his friends to hire him in the computer department, blaming Brian's criminal record on those terrible teenage years and he was now a reformed man. This was borne out by his first year of employment when his work effort was exemplary and his record unblemished. That was because he had discovered a huge hole in the bank's financial security system and devised a plan to capitalize upon it.

When foreign exchange transactions are made, unless the conversion results in an exact amount, there is always a very small decimal amount that gets rounded up. When you are dealing in billions of dollars on a daily basis it is surprising how quickly small decimal amounts can amass into a large sum of money. The beauty of it was that as far as audit trails and balances were concerned it was undetectable. Over the course of six months Brian embezzled money from the bank's system, initially, by transferring those decimal amounts to one of his own accounts. He could have probably continued along these lines for some considerable time without being detected, but then Brian unwisely decided to go for broke.

The day before he handed in his resignation, citing that a better opportunity had been offered to him, he went in for the kill. He knew that because of his position there was a strong possibility that once he had informed the bank that he was leaving they might release him immediately for security reasons. So Brian had to enter the transaction that he expected would net him a huge pay day the day before he handed in his notice. Brian had already selected an account with a seven digit balance and thousands of transactions being credited and debited to it on a daily basis. He had been monitoring the activity on the account for a couple of weeks and felt it was an excellent candidate. His thinking was that with that many transactions taking place it would be at least a couple of days before the debit was questioned; by then he would be out of the country. Unfortunately for Brian, as fate would have it, the company that owned the account was under surveillance by the RCMP because of suspected criminal activities. Consequently, as soon as the transaction was posted by the computer that evening, software that had been installed to identify potentially suspicious activity traced the source of the debit to Brian's work terminal. The next morning he logged in to check the balance of the account that was to receive the embezzled funds. Satisfied the transfer had taken place he promptly handed in his resignation, which is precisely when they arrested him. The authorities were able to retrieve the embezzled funds for the transaction that was his undoing. After further investigation of Brian's activities they discovered the software that was transferring the decimal amounts but they were never able to recover that money which had been safely ensconced in a numbered Swiss bank account.

After his conviction, while he was incarcerated in the Rotunda, he was contacted by a Gracie Brown. Gracie was studying to be a journalist, and she was interested in writing a paper on Brian for her thesis. She contacted the warden and he gave her permission to visit Brian, if he agreed. Why wouldn't Brian want to have regular visits from a beautiful young woman? So, he agreed to some interviews with her which were then authorized by the warden. Even so, the authorities were still not aware that it was Gracie who had aided and abetted Brian's escape. Brian and Gracie had used false passports to leave the country so nobody was aware that Gracie had actually left and they certainly wouldn't be looking for her marriage notice in the newspapers. It wasn't until Dexter Davis received Brian's email that the authorities were alerted to the subterfuge; even then, they were only interested in Brian's relocation and Gracie was lost under most people's radar.

Brian and Gracie had been successful with their planning to date and they were about to embark on the next phase of their lives. They had not, however, escaped the attention of everyone in Brazil.

CHAPTER 5

A Meeting

It was mid-morning on a beautiful sunny day which found Brian and Gracie walking calmly down a boulevard enjoying some window shopping after drinking expressos and eating pastries at a local bistro. Just ahead of them an expensive black limo slowed and stopped. A tall man in a smart, tailored, expensive looking suit got out of the passenger side, walked to the back of the car and onto the pavement's side where he opened the rear door. As the couple neared the man he indicated to them that he was ushering them into the car. Brian and Gracie ignored him and tried to walk through the crowd and past the man but the width of the sidewalk was narrowed because of the open door and the man standing beside it, who was quite the obstacle. Although the man was displaying a very charming smile he was wearing sun glasses so it was difficult to judge his real demeanor until he spoke, "come, you have a meeting to attend." His English was good but flaked with a Portuguese accent. His voice was pleasant and inviting but there was a hint of menace in the tone.

"Er, no thanks, I think we'll pass." Brian replied pleasantly and he attempted to shield Gracie from the man by walking between her and their oppressor as they went to pass the open car door. But the man just blocked their path and he nonchalantly unbuttoned his jacket to reveal a shoulder holster that wasn't empty.

"You're not going to intimidate me," Brian said, "you won't use that gun in a crowded thoroughfare like this. How far do you think you'd get?"

"My apologies Mr. Beasley. I am not wishing to intimidate you I am simply trying to show you how serious we are about getting you to your meeting in a punctual fashion." At the sound of his name Brian realized there was more to this than a coincidence and it was unlikely it was a kidnapping; there would be far too many witnesses around.

"I'm sorry," Brian said, "I appear to have forgotten about this meeting. Who exactly is it with again?"

"That's understandable Mr. Beasley," the man replied in a matter-of-fact fashion, "it was only arranged a very short time ago but you may be proud to know you are a key attendee."

"But you still haven't mentioned who it is with." Brian said, still exhibiting a casual relaxed attitude as if this was a chat between two old friends.

"You will be introduced at the meeting. Come, our host does not like to be kept waiting." The man said.

"But what if I declined to attend?" Brian asked.

"I'm afraid it is not an option Mr. Beasley." The man said in a much more serious tone and he indicated with a wave of his arm for the couple to enter the car.

"Gracie, I'll see you later at the hangout." The hangout was a small bar in one of the downtown hotels. This was a previously arranged meeting point in the event of an unforeseen emergency if they somehow got split up and considered it too risky to return to their apartment.

"No, I insist. Miss Brown must accompany you. Have no fear, she will be pleasantly entertained while you are attending your meeting." The man said, "please, come, you will be safe, I can assure you and afterwards you will be returned to your apartment," and he smiled pleasantly at Gracie. Both Brian and Gracie exchanged glances and he was seriously considering making a bolt for it but that would really only delay the inevitable. If these people could pick them out of a crowd that easily, what hiding place did they really have in Rio and the next time they may not be as friendly. So, reluctantly, Brian climbed into the car closely followed by Gracie.

Brian and Gracie had no idea in which direction they were headed. They just sat silently in the back of the car with Gracie hanging on to Brian's arm as though her life depended on it. The windows were so darkly tinted they couldn't see outside, negating any attempt to memorize their route. There was a small light that provided some illumination at the back of the car but they couldn't hear nor see the occupants in the front of the car due to a thick steel divider that separated them. Brian was certain this wasn't the first time this car had been used to transport passengers for nefarious purposes.

Finally the car began to slow and they could hear gravel crunching beneath the tires as it came to a halt. The same man opened the rear door and waited for Brian and Gracie to exit the car.

"This is Eduardo." The man said pointing to an immaculately dressed butler, "he will take you to your host." The butler bowed, smiled and with a wave of his hand indicated that they should be seated on the back seat of the golf cart parked in front of them. The cart was a little more than your run of the mill golf cart that you rent on the links. This one had a bar, plush seats and came equipped with a colorful Bimini top. A quick check of their surroundings revealed a large well maintained mansion surrounded by immaculately groomed grounds. Once they were seated the butler got into the driver's seat and proceeded to drive slowly to the rear of the mansion. As Eduardo drove them, Brian and Gracie were able to look at the grounds more thoroughly. They were impeccably maintained with beautiful flowering trees and bushes. Hibiscus were in full bloom, palm trees, bougainvillea of various colors lined the gravel path as they continued travelling around the house. Towards the back of the house they began to see a small lake that was as long as the width of the house. The lake was teeming with birds of all species, probably with their wings clipped so that they were permanent residents; nevertheless, it provided a beautiful backdrop for the patio they were now approaching. From the patio a stone block path led to a spacious hot tub underneath a tiki-styled cabana. The path encircled the hot tub which in turn led to a beautifully landscaped pool resplendent with rockeries containing waterfalls, fountains and even more exotic flowers. Gracie thought it was all spectacular and she was trying to identify every bird and every flower with a keen interest. Brian on the other hand was more focused on a very large man sitting on a swing chair underneath a voluminous sun umbrella.

The cart came to a stop and the butler got off and with a beaming smile directed them to seats immediately in front of the large man. The man had been surrounded by bikini clad women but as Brian and Gracie approached, the ladies were dismissed and immediately disappeared through large French doors at the back of the mansion.

"Welcome to my home," the man said with sincerity in a deep commanding voice and a bow of his large, bald head, "my name is Diego Martinez. I trust you had a pleasant drive." Without waiting for an answer he continued. "I know all about you Mr. Beasley. I have been following your, let's say, career with interest. Now can I offer you any refreshments?" Diego Martinez's English was perfect, not a trace of an accent whatsoever. His demeanor gave Brian the impression of absolute self-confidence and an appreciation that he was the type of man who got what he wanted.

Brian had heard of Diego Martinez, he was **the man** in Rio. He controlled the drug trafficking, prostitution rings and generally all the major crime that took place in both Rio and Sao Paulo. During his trial for the bank job Brian had been incarcerated with a Brazilian trying to fight an extradition order back to his homeland. The man told Brian about Martinez, his dealings and the details of his mansion which he claimed he had seen first-hand. The mansion, the man explained to Brian, was situated on the outskirts of Rio, surrounded by a massive wall with an electrified fence on top of it. A large well maintained hedge on the inside of the wall was strategically placed to hide the wall and provide some natural beauty for the residents and guests to look at. The grounds were patrolled by armed guards 24/7 and entry into the mansion itself would be as difficult as getting into Fort Knox. What's more, Diego Martinez rarely left his property: why would he? All his business transactions could be arranged at his mansion and he had all the good things of life at his fingertips. Although he didn't drink alcohol or did drugs he had a penchant for good food and beautiful women. So at any given time, fine food was always available, prepared to perfection by a top chef which was then handed to beautiful, scantily clad women who acted as waitresses. From where Brian was sitting the description the man had provided appeared to be 100% accurate.

"No thanks Mr. Martinez. What I would like to know is what this is all about." Brian replied.

"Ah, direct to the point, a man of action. I like that Mr. Beasley."

"Call me Brian." Brian replied.

"Certainly Brian." Martinez replied with a slight smile. He then raised his arm and snapped his fingers. From nowhere a man appeared and Martinez introduced him as his head grounds man.

"Pedro has been with me for many years and he knows everything about my plantation." Martinez said, "Miss Brown, perhaps you would like to accompany Pedro as he carries out his rounds. I am sure you will find it very interesting, knowing your love of nature. Ask him anything you like, his English is very good. Not as good as mine but still very good." Martinez said, in a way that was more of an instruction than an idea. Gracie glanced at Brian, he nodded his acquiescence. Brian knew it wasn't a question, it was a ruse to leave Brian and Diego Martinez all alone. Whatever it was that brought him here was about to be revealed.

"Mr. Beasley, sorry, Brian. I keep my ear very close to the ground here in Rio. Of course, I have people who assist me in this endeavor, good people in high places. But it never ceases to amaze me how certain people can put innocuous pieces of data together and find a diamond in the rough." Martinez paused to have a sip of some freshly squeezed orange juice before continuing. "This was the case with my good friend David Deluca, the gentleman who escorted you here in the car as a matter of fact." On cue, Deluca came towards them from the patio doors of the mansion carrying what appeared to be one of those security wands they use for seeking out concealed objects on passengers at airports.

"If you wouldn't mind standing Mr. Beasley." Deluca said as he came towards him. "Arms outstretched if you please." Brian did as he was asked although he was somewhat surprised as he was dressed casually in a t-shirt, shorts and sneakers. If he was wearing a wire or some type of listening device there weren't too many places he could conceal it. Martinez may have sensed his surprise.

"We can't be too careful Brian." Martinez said before he continued with his intro. "David had come across your wedding announcement in the newspaper. As a man of the world he was aware of your breakout from prison as you are one of the greatest embezzlers in modern time. He put two and two together, as you say, and followed it up as he felt it was all too much of a coincidence. Once he had confirmed it was you he brought it to my attention and voilà, here you are."

"Well I am very flattered Mr. Martinez but I still don't see how I can help you. You see I have made enough money to keep me in the lifestyle I want for the rest of my life and I don't need to take any further risks to jeopardize that. I'm happy to keep below the radar" Brian replied nonchalantly.

"I understand that fully Brian. Call me Diego by the way, all my friends do." Martinez replied. "But what did you make during your crime wave, a few million?"

"Maybe." Brian replied unwilling to disclose any details.

"Much of which has been used up in expenses to finance your new life here. Isn't that right?" Martinez said. Brian thought he was bluffing, he couldn't possibly know exactly how much he had stashed away as a result of his crimes nor could he know how much he had been forced to spend to date. But there was some semblance of truth in the observations. Brian didn't reply so Martinez continued quite nonchalantly.

"What if I told you that I have a job for someone with your expertise to participate in a plot to steal the equivalent of half a billion U.S. dollars in a single afternoon?"

CHAPTER 6

The Deal

Brian was totally dumbfounded. He knew Martinez was a player but this much? "Did you say half a billion? Five hundred million U.S. dollars?" Brian asked incredulously.

"Possibly more if everything goes to plan and all of it cash comprising of bills that are untraceable." Martinez replied with all seriousness. "Has that got your attention Brian? Is that something you would come out of retirement for?"

"How exactly?" Brian was all ears now, his interest piqued and he was dying to know just how Martinez expected to pull this one off. "Where exactly is all that money coming from?"

"You sound surprised Brian" Martinez said. "Don't be. Brazil has one of the biggest economies in the world, there is plenty of money to be had. What is more a recent report from the World Bank stated that Brazil has more Automated Teller Machines, or ATMs as we call them nowadays, than any other county in the world. It was this statistic that first gave me the idea for the robbery. You see the ATMs are where all the money will be coming from."

"You're going to extract the equivalent of a half of a billion US dollars from ATMs," Brian replied, unimpressed, and let out a laugh, "ha, you've got to be kidding me. That would take forever."

"On the contrary." Martinez said undaunted and he began to explain. "As you know, Brazil is hosting the summer games this year. After the group games for the football teams. Wait, you refer to it as soccer, after the group games for the soccer, the first of the elimination rounds are scheduled for 3:00 PM on a Saturday, here in Rio. You may not be aware of the fanatical support that exists for our national soccer team but I can assure you the streets of every town and city in this country will be deserted at that time. Roads will be void of traffic, banks and stores will be empty and in many cases closed for the duration of the game.

At 3:00 PM as the teams kick-off I will have operatives assigned to various zones and they will hit the ATMs with specially produced bank cards. The cards will be entered into the machines, the ATM will recognize the card and will not require any further entering of any data like PIN numbers. The ATMs will recognize the cards and they will merely respond by spewing out their contents into the waiting hands of my people. It is estimated that it should take no more than ten minutes to clear out the machines at each site, give or take. Depending of course on how many ATMs are at the site; some may have two, some as many as ten. We expect each operative to hit at least five sites in their zone, beginning with the ones with the most ATMs and to continue until 4:30 PM. The actual time, however, is open to debate; it may be a little later. That is for the team to decide. Regardless, on completion the operatives will transport the funds, obtained in their transactions, in bags, to a distribution point. On completion of the drop offs, the monies received at the distribution point will then be transported to a central location. The money will then be loaded onto a truck and delivered here to the mansion. However, simultaneously, we also plan to have operatives working in Sao Paulo, Salvador and Brasilia; for them, instead of a truck, delivery will be made to the mansion by commercial cargo helicopters. You may have noticed the helipad the other side of the mansion as you rode in the shuttle to meet me. Estimated time of the arrivals of truck and helicopters is expected to be as soon as possible after the completion of the soccer game. Only then will the banks even be aware they have been cleaned out."

In Sao Paulo we expect to relieve approximately 10,000 ATM machines of their contents that would have been filled to the maximum. Likewise in Rio, but fewer machines: maybe 6,000. In Brasilia and Salvador another 2,000 each. Each ATM can hold as much as 200,000

Brazilian REAL, possibly more. That's the equivalent of approximately US$ 50,000." Martinez paused to have another sip of orange juice and a bite of a freshly prepared Danish. "Of course, with the best planning in the world it would be difficult to hit every single ATM in the time available but we will do our best. We will only be concentrating on banks, we won't be touching those single ATMs in convenience stores and other small institutions; too much hassle." Martinez stopped talking for a moment and then asked, "so Brian, what do you think?"

For a minute, Brian was speechless. Then the questions came to his head all at once. "That's a lot to take in. There's so much that could go wrong and how are you going to get that many operatives to visit every ATM in those cities?" Brian asked.

"Trust me, I can get the operatives." Martinez calmly replied.

"Trust is the operative word here, excuse the pun. You will need hundreds of them. With that many people involved how can you guarantee one of them won't squeal to the police?" Brian said.

"You are obviously unaware of my reputation Brian. Squealing, as you say, will not occur." Martinez replied but what was unsaid said everything. "I am planning to use around two hundred and fifty operatives and they will be paid handsomely for their efforts, instantly I might add."

"But what is to stop them putting their hand in the till, as it were. And take a little more than they had been promised?" Brian questioned. "Trying to reconcile every operative with every ATM with the amounts in every bag would be almost impossible."

"I fully expect some indiscretions." Martinez agreed. "You must also remember that some of these operatives do not exactly have a degree in mathematics. And, if they think by taking a few extra REALs they get one up on the man then so be it. Let them have their day, the profit margin for us will nevertheless be very large," Martinez added.

"The drop off points, why do they need to go to a central site" Brian asked. "Why can't they just drive straight here?"

"Good question Brian." Martinez replied tilting his head slightly in acknowledgement. "At the central site will be a vehicle that enters these grounds every day, except Sundays. Specifically the daily delivery of fresh fruit and vegetables to help feed the many people who work here.

Comings and goings on this property are often closely monitored. If three unexplained vehicles arrive here the same day a substantial amount of money disappeared it may create some unwanted attention."

"But won't the arrival of three helicopters create some unwanted attention?" Brian asked.

"Not unduly, we have a large helipad here," Martinez explained, "helicopters come and go all the time."

"What about the time differences, will they be a factor?" Brian asked.

"Not at all. Our schedules will be based on Rio time, as 3:00 PM our time is the kick-off. That will be our base time." Martinez replied casually.

"But you can't guarantee Brazil will even make the play-offs. What happens if they fail to come out of their group?" Brian asked what he thought was a reasonable question. Diego topped eating his pastry and looked indignantly at Brian.

"That will not happen Brian – they will qualify I can assure you." Martinez said convincingly.

"O.K. I get how you can control the soccer results. I get you can put that many operatives on the streets but how the hell can you get the ATMs to just hand over their entire contents? Brian asked thinking this time he would stump the big king pin.

"Oh I can't Brian." Martinez replied quite easily. "That's why you're here."

CHAPTER 7

The Plan

Brian sat with his mouth agape and his eyes wide open looking at the big man. "No, I think you have the wrong man, this is beyond my expertise." Brian said smiling and shaking his head from side to side.

On the contrary Brian. You underestimate yourself, you are the perfect man for the job." Martinez countered.

"Think of it, half a billion dollars. Your take would be twenty million. Think what you could do with twenty million dollars." Martinez said, continuing to munch on his Danish.

"Only twenty? If I did the job I would want at least a hundred million." Brian stated.

"Now, now, Brian let's not get too greedy. After all, that's what got you caught last time wasn't it? If you had of stopped at $2 million you would have got away scot free. But no, one more transaction and wham – they got you." Martinez said all too smugly. "Ten percent, that's fifty million that will be your take. More than enough I feel. I am running all the risks, organizing the troops, the planning and the buy offs. I also have a large up-front expenditure. All you have to do is write a few programs."

"Precisely. Without me you couldn't do it could you?" Brian said jostling for an upper hand in the negotiation process.

"Now it is you who underestimate me Brian." Martinez retorted. "This isn't something I have been thinking about since we found out you were in the country. I have been planning this ever since Brazil was awarded the games. Your availability is a bonus." Martinez had finished his Danish and was selecting another one from a large silver platter full of them while Brian was given time to think about that.

"But I would need to get access to the Brazilian banking systems. I have no idea how to do that." Brian protested.

"Again Brian. You completely underestimate me." Martinez said, feigning indignation. "A command post has already been set up with an experienced systems team that will provide you with all the expertise, equipment and facilities you will need. It will also be the central site for the drop offs here in Rio. You will be able to monitor the transactions as they occur. In addition, I will ensure you are provided with names of IT personnel in various banks who will grant you access to their systems and any additional information you may need. However, from the little experience I have gleaned from discussions with various technical personnel my understanding is that there is standard software that each bank has that directs a request to the appropriate bank on the system. Much like a traffic cop. If that traffic cop could be compromised to direct the appropriate instructions immediately back to the ATM it would bypass most of the communications and also save a little time. So, once you have written the program, it could be uploaded to every bank. But I don't want to cloud your brain with my ideas. You will know what to do."

"What about upgrades?" Brian said, still trying to find a hole in the plan. "Banks carry out software updates and hardware upgrades all the time. We may have all the software ready then 'whammo', changes are made and we're screwed."

"Because of the games and the anticipated extra usage of all the ATMs there is a freeze on any software updates, except emergency fixes of course, from a month prior to the opening ceremony to one month after the closing ceremony." Martinez assured Brian. The fact that Martinez knew this, and the terminology he used, was enough to blow the wind completely out of Brian's sails. As one of his best friends used to say, 'his gast was flabbered'. All he could do now was just try the petulant angle.

"And what if I don't what to do it?" Brian said defiantly. "I am on egg shells here as it is with a potential extradition order hanging over my head. If this goes down I would be a prime suspect. If a multi-million dollar heist caused by a computer hack goes down they'd kick me out of the country as quick as look at me, guilty or not."

"With a little plastic surgery and a new identity you could go anywhere in the world and that's something I could assist you with, out of my own personal expenses." Martinez said nonchalantly as he continued chewing on his second Danish. "I also know some excellent cosmetic surgeons who would ask no questions."

"Nope. Too much of a risk. As you said, I got too greedy last time. I'm content with what I have, I think I'll pass on your lucrative yet flattering offer." Brian said with some finality. At this remark Martinez slowly placed the Danish he was eating on a fine bone china side plate. He tilted his large frame forward and looked directly into Brian's eyes before saying with not a little malice, "Brian, my dear boy. You don't understand, this is not an offer."

CHAPTER 8

The Partnership

Martinez sat back in his chair but continued to stare at Brian. After a short pause he resumed the demolition of his Danish and began speaking again, returning to the eloquent, charming tone he had been using up until his last statement. "The little extradition order that is sure to arrive in the next few weeks could get buried in red tape OR," Martinez paused for effect, "it could be fast-tracked to fulfillment before you could obtain Brazilian citizenship." He then turned slightly and pointed to Gracie looking over the lake with his grounds man. "That young lady, she is quite beautiful. With you gone she would be left here, all alone, with no one to take care of her or to support her. What is she to you? Why of course, you are married aren't you, to another woman? So technically she would have to be your mistress." Martinez said matter of fact. "Well, if word got out that this married woman had been the mistress of an extradited felon I'm afraid the local women would frown upon that. I would be forced to take the poor girl under my wing for her own protection." His voice trailed off as he continued to lewdly watch Gracie pointing enthusiastically at the birds on the man-made lake. There was a lingering pause as Brian turned his attention to Gracie, who was in deep discussion with the grounds man. Brian saw her standing there with her long hair blowing in the warm breeze and he felt a cold pang in the pit of his stomach at the thought of what Martinez may be capable of. Just at that moment she turned to see the two men staring at her and she reacted by waving vigorously to them. Brian returned her wave. He knew he was beat and without turning to look at Martinez, Brian spoke.

"When do I start?" Brian said reluctantly.

Without hesitation, as if Martinez had anticipated what Brian would say, he replied, "here, take this," and he passed Brian a cell phone together with a battery charger, "make sure it is always turned on and fully charged. I may need to contact you for some reason, day or night. There is one number in the contact list; if you need anything, anything at all, feel free to call that number, anytime of day." Martinez offered pleasantly. "Just be careful what you say on the call. The number is unlisted and unlikely to be tapped but I cannot guarantee it. One more thing: nothing in writing, ever. That means no emails, texts or social media. Any time you need to talk to me, use the phone to arrange a meeting or contact David, he will be your liaison." Martinez paused and smiled, "now, David will escort you home in the limo. Why don't you and Gracie relax for a few days? See the sights, go to the beach. I will give you the names of some good restaurants where you will be well treated. How does that sound?"

"Sounds pretty good to me." Brian responded. "We have had a pretty hectic few days and it would be nice just to relax and not have to worry about anything."

"Precisely." Martinez said enthusiastically. "Recharge the old batteries then, shall we say a week from Monday? You will be picked up to be taken to your new offices where you will be able to begin work on the biggest heist in world history. That's something we can both look forward to."

As if on cue the grounds man brought Gracie back to the patio and after a few fond farewells Eduardo took them back to the front of the mansion in the souped-up golf cart. Brian and Gracie were returned to their apartment in the same limo that brought them to Martinez's house, only this time the heavy divider was down and Deluca sat in the rear of the car chatting with them like an old lost friend. He provided them with suggestions on where to visit, which tourist traps to avoid and a short history of the city and peoples of Rio. Occasionally he would ask his driver for suggestions or confirmation of various facts but other than that, his driver said nothing. On arriving at their apartment building the driver quickly left the car and came around to open the door for Brian and Gracie to exit the limo. This was the first time they had actually seen the man outside of the car. He was a huge, solid fellow with a bald head and eyes as black as coals. There was no doubt he would also be packing some sort of fire arm under the loose fitting jacket he was wearing. Brian said later to Gracie that he thought that based on the size of the man he could fit a high powered rifle under there and nobody would notice. The man didn't smile as Brian and Gracie got out of the limo but he did bow his head slightly in a way of bidding farewell. Immediately following them out was Deluca.

"So, 9:00 AM sharp, a week from Monday. O.K.?" Asked Deluca to which Brian nodded his head in agreement. Then there were hugs and handshakes all around as though Deluca and his driver were departing after a friendly get together instead of them being the henchmen of the top gangster in Brazil. Passersby were looking askance wondering if Brian and Gracie were royalty or celebrities, instead of an embezzler and his moll.

As soon as Deluca's limo had departed Brian turned to Gracie and whispered, "say nothing incriminating when we get up to the apartment. I bet you a dime to a doughnut that our apartment is bugged." Brian had also put his hand to his mouth so that anyone watching could not lip-read what he was saying. It made Gracie aware that this chance meeting with Martinez was not exactly scheduled to discuss flower arranging classes, but she merely took it in her stride.

While Brian and Gracie returned to their apartment Deluca and his driver returned to the mansion where Martinez instructed him to put both Brian and Gracie under 24 hours a day surveillance. He also wanted to be kept appraised of their bugged conversations, whereabouts and especially the people they came in contact with.

CHAPTER 9

Meeting the Staff

Those few days between the meeting and Brian having to go to work for Martinez were the best Brian and Gracie had ever spent in their lives. Martinez was good on his word and whenever they arrived at a restaurant and told the maître de that Diego M. had recommended their establishment they were treated like royalty. They rented a car and visited nature parks, snorkeled over spectacular reefs, drove by many of the games' venues and relaxed on some of the best beaches in the world. They took the cable car up Sugarloaf Mountain, a must-do when in Rio. Naturally one of the highlights was their visit to Tijuca Forest National Park, site of one of the most famous statues in the world, Christ the Redeemer on top of the Corcovado Mountain. Gracie was absolutely thrilled to witness this modern wonder of the world first-hand; its art deco style fascinated her. She was equally impressed with the painted murals in the fairytale-like Mayrink chapel situated in the same National Park. The Cascatinha waterfall was also something to behold and while they hiked through the park Gracie was constantly armed with binoculars and a bird identification book. Gracie was in her element trying to identify the various, colorful breeds of her feathered friends.

They had enjoyed themselves thoroughly, but all too quickly it was Sunday evening and the fun had to stop. They returned the car to the rental agency and discussed the advantages and disadvantages of owning a car in Rio, however, a pleasant surprise the next morning took the decision out of their hands. At precisely 9:00 AM on Monday morning as Brian was drinking the dregs of his morning coffee he looked out of his apartment window and saw David Deluca waving to him as he stood beside a brand new Honda SUV. Deluca was dressed, as usual, in an immaculate suit and the obligatory sunglasses. Brian felt a little underdressed for the occasion, wearing a T-shirt, shorts and sneakers. Brian turned and gave Gracie a kiss and a hug. She wished him luck then he went out the door, trotted down the stairs and out onto the street to be heartily greeted by Deluca.

"No limo this morning David?" Brian asked with feigned disappointment. "I thought I would be given the royal treatment on my first day."

"Mr. Beasley, you stab me in the heart." Deluca said, pretending to be mortally horrified by Brian's comment. "This is so much better. Mr. Martinez is not only supplying you with this fine automobile he is also giving you this credit card to purchase gas anytime you need it." Deluca handed Brian the credit card and a slip of paper with the PIN number written on it. "And of course, any other expenses you may incur."

"Wow that is very generous of Mr. Martinez." Said Brian with genuine surprise. "I'm amazed he would do something like that."

"Don't be. Mr. Martinez looks after all his people." Deluca said with some reverence. "He finds he gets better productivity and loyalty with a cup of sugar than a bitter pill. Hey, but I must warn you, play games with Mr. Martinez and you will be receiving a little more than a bitter pill if you know what I mean." Then Deluca tossed the keys to the Honda over to Brian.

"Good to know," Brian replied quietly as he caught the keys.

They entered the car with Brian in the driver's seat. He made the necessary adjustments to the seat and mirrors before familiarizing himself with the workings of his brand-new car. Deluca had already entered the address of the command post into the built-in GPS. This is where Brian would be spending most of the next few months. The engine was still running; Deluca had not turned off the ignition, so once Brian felt he was ready to leave he moved the automatic gear shift to 'Drive', checked his mirrors to make sure the road was all clear and drove on the route dictated to him by the melodious voice of the Latin-sounding lady with the erotic English accent on the GPS.

According to the GPS they arrived at their destination some forty five minutes later. Not bad considering the traffic, the wild Rio drivers, the fact that Brian had not driven in congested traffic for some time and his unfamiliarity with the car. It was just the final destination that Brian was questioning. He was expecting to see at least an office block or tower in the middle of a bustling business district with cafes, pubs and restaurants nearby. What he was looking at was a strip of derelict buildings in a remote area of the seedy side of town. The buildings appeared to be old workshops, car garages and storage rooms. Deluca, who was smiling broadly, indicated where Brian should park. There were three other cars parked outside and Brian eased the car behind one of them and turned off the engine.

"What the hell is this?" Brian asked. His mind was racing a hundred miles a minute. He was supposed to hack into some of the most sophisticated, secure networks on the planet and he was going to be housed in buildings that looked as though a good wind would blow them away.

"All is not what it appears." Deluca said, beginning to laugh now. "Let me show you the command post and you will see what I mean." Deluca continued as he opened the car door and started to walk towards one of the broken down looking doors. Brian left the car to follow him, standing a little way back in case the door fell off its hinges. Deluca opened a Judas gate and held the door open for Brian to enter. Brian entered with some trepidation but when he stepped through he felt like Alice walking through the looking glass into wonderland.

"Now, this is what I'm talking about." Brian whispered. He had walked into a climate-controlled well-lit room and on the far wall were banks of computers, servers, modems and printers blinking and whirring in perfect harmony to his ears. There were offices with modern furniture on the two opposing walls, all equipped with personal computers and telephones. There was a gantry leading up to another level that housed a fully-equipped kitchen, a dining area and washrooms. It was if a whole modern module had been equipped and pushed into the hole that was the derelict building. Brian was duly impressed.

"Come, I will introduce you to your team and then show you around." Deluca said. There were three men in white lab coats and were wearing latex gloves, which Brian thought was a little strange. The men were standing by what Brian assumed was the main console and they were beaming with anticipated pleasure to meet the great embezzler and the newest member of their team.

"Brian," said Deluca as he was putting an arm around the shoulders of a diminutive man who was grinning from ear to ear, highlighting his friendly dark brown eyes, "this is Filipe Gomez, he is your technical expert. He takes care of all the equipment, upgrades, servicing. There's nothing he doesn't know about these machines. If there is a superior anything on the market he will get it. So believe me, everything here is state-of-the-art. You couldn't go and buy anything better."

"Filipe." Brian acknowledged the man as he shook his hand.

"Olá senor Brian." Filipe replied.

"Filipe's English is not very good I'm afraid, but we expect you will be conversing in 'technicalese' anyway and over the next few weeks I am sure his English will improve, as will your Portuguese." Deluca offered in the way of an apology. He moved along slightly to introduce the next man in the line. He was tall, dark and once his smile disappeared he looked very serious.

"Here we have José Henriques." Deluca said, "José is your software expert and your right-hand man. He will be instrumental in obtaining access to any banking system you need and he can assist in the programming, if necessary. José was originally the young man we were going to use to do what you are now being asked to do. So he is very familiar with the plan." Deluca patted José on the back as the man shook hands with Brian.

"'ello, it is very good to meet you." José said with a strong accent in what was obviously a rehearsed speech.

"José has been practicing his English with me and it is coming along very well. I'm sure you will have no communication problems. Deluca said patting José on the back once more.

"Finally, we have the most important man on the team." Deluca said and everyone laughed and looked at the last man to be introduced.

It was unlikely that Filipe understood what Deluca had said exactly but he was in on the joke.

"This is Osvaldo and he is responsible for keeping this place clean and making sure the refrigerator is well stocked with food, drink, anything you need. He is here during the day to prepare your lunches and dinners, if necessary. He is, I might add, an excellent cook and it is only a matter of time before Mr. Martinez calls him to the mansion to work there. So, enjoy while you can." As Deluca said this he stood behind the man with his hands on his shoulders which accentuated just how short Osvaldo was. But he didn't seem to care; he thought it was all very amusing.

"Good morning Mr. Beasley, welcome to the office." Osvaldo said in very good English. Ironically, the one with the good English was the cook. He would be useful for any translation issues, Brian thought before acknowledging Osvaldo's warm greeting.

"Hi, nice to meet you," Brian responded politely.

"Osvaldo's name means 'divine power' in Latin, so be very careful Mr. Beasley." Deluca joked and everyone burst out laughing.

"What's with the latex gloves? Brian said pointing to the gloves on Filipe's hands. "I can understand Osvaldo wearing them for hygiene purposes but the others?"

"Additional security. No fingerprints or DNA." Deluca replied with a smile. "Mr. Martinez insists every precaution should be taken, just in case." Once Brian digested that surprising piece of information Deluca shouted jokingly, "that's it then. Back to work." Deluca clapped his hands and shooed the three men off. He then indicated to Brian to follow him up the stairs to the next level for an inspection of the rest of the place. He gave Brian the full tour. In the washrooms there was even a shower resplendent with expensive soaps, shampoos and lotions. The kitchen was equipped with just about every appliance you could think of and the refrigerator/freezer was well-stocked with everything you would need for breakfast, lunch, dinner, and snacks.

"Everything but a bottle of beer," Brian noted as he looked inside the large refrigerator at the veritable cornucopia of food and drink.

"Special instruction from Mr. Martinez, no alcohol" Deluca explained, "one rule that should be respected I'm afraid." Not wanting to dwell on Martinez's hypocrisy, a man who pushes drugs and illicit booze but is an abstainer himself Brian thought, so he closed the refrigerator door and quickly changed the subject.

"How trustworthy are these three guys?" Brian asked quietly.

"Absolute." Replied Deluca without hesitation. "Filipe and Osvaldo have worked for Mr. Martinez since they were children. They were guttersnipes in the slums of Rio and he rescued them, helped their families and gave them careers. Their loyalty is guaranteed. As for José, he joined the corporation a few months ago but his credentials are impeccable and I wouldn't worry about him."

"And this place, how secure is it?" Brian asked as he looked at the ceiling and the walls of the converted workshop."

"You may not have noticed but there was a security camera on a telegraph pole on the road that led to this line of buildings." Deluca replied. "The only road in. There are two more cameras centered on these buildings. At the back of us is the Rio Guandu and just wild, thick brush on the other side of it. The Guandu is one of the rivers that provides water to the city. The fact that it is seriously polluted, containing all sorts of raw sewage and industrial waste is neither here nor there but you certainly will not get anybody swimming across it to get to here. There is no one living within a kilometer of this place on either side of the river. What is more, if any trespassers are seen by our security people monitoring the cameras a team of, shall we say, security guards would be dispatched and they would be here within a short time. So, yes, it is considered very secure."

"Wow!" Brian said, quite impressed, "it seems you have thought of everything."

"We like to think so." Deluca said proudly.

"What is more, these buildings are all owned by Mr. Martinez - maybe not in his name, but he has total control of them. He has owned them for the last year, everyone around here knows that and they stay away. Next door to you is an old garage, where they used to carry out motor repairs, oil changes and engine rebuilds. Nobody ever goes in there; it smells of old oil and gas. It has six concrete bays dug out of the ground with steel doors on top of them that time has rusted and they are not safe to walk across. That's why we call the building the 'pits', a nice play on words don't you think? On the other side of the command post is another room but nobody ever uses that except when we have certain things that, shall we say, need to be dealt with."

"Dealt with?" Brian asked.

"Yes dealt with. But don't trouble yourself with that." Deluca said using his arm to brush away the remark as if he was flapping at an imaginary insect. But unfortunately, it was something that did trouble Brian.

CHAPTER 10

Getting Started

Brian heard a quiet buzzing sound and Deluca instinctively looked down at the phone on his belt. It must have been a call from Deluca's driver as Deluca said, "now, I will leave you, I believe my ride has just arrived. If you need anything, anything at all, let José know, he knows how to get hold of me. I would prefer you to take that route rather than call Mr. Martinez direct as it makes me look bad you understand. Anyway, good luck." He bowed his head slightly and held out his hand. Brian shook it and with that Deluca bounded down the stairs and he was gone. Brian lingered at the top of the stairs to contemplate for a moment, elbows leaning on the green, gantry railing. Then he decided it was time to start work so he went down the stairs and carried out a quick recce of the offices before walking over to check out the equipment. Although what they were doing was totally illegal the planning involved was tremendous and the gig had to be treated as if it were a major computer project, which indeed is what it was. It required resources, planning, timelines as well as the usual project stages, analysis, design, programming and testing. He decided to have an impromptu meeting with his newly hired staff. He had noticed a meeting room with a flip chart, a white board and markers. He walked over to the door of the meeting room and called the three men over, they came in and sat down, still a little apprehensive. Filipe handed Brian a pair of latex gloves, Brian thanked him and Filipe bobbed his head in acknowledgement.

Brian had a little difficulty putting on the gloves but he persevered and Osvaldo assured him it was a knack that he would soon develop.

"O.K." Brian said, clapping his hands and smiling at the dull thud provided by the gloves, "let's get started. The first thing I want to do is understand all the critical activities necessary to get this job done. That includes the positioning of the operatives and any other outside dependencies we may have." As Brian spoke Osvaldo, who was strategically seated between Filipe and José, quietly translated. "And don't assume I will think of everything. This is a team effort so do not be afraid to speak up if you disagree with anything or you think a detail is missing. The devil is in the details and we cannot afford to miss a thing." Brian stopped to let Osvaldo's translation catch up and for the information to be digested before continuing. "Now, you are probably aware that one of Mr. Martinez's instructions is 'nothing in writing'. So, all of our communications will be verbal. But, during the course of this project it will be impossible to work without some specifications and documents to assist us at every stage. However, nothing is to leave this building and nothing will ever be sent to anyone, anywhere. In fact, I want the creation of all documentation to be restricted to PCs that have no internet connection so they cannot possibly be hacked. Is that understood?" Brian paused as Osvaldo translated and waited for a short discussion to finish between the three men. Filipe then said something which Osvaldo translated for Brian's purpose.

"Filipe will ensure the PCs in the offices are disconnected from any network and bring in some more printers to be hard wired connected." Osvaldo said.

"Great idea, Filipe, so then we can just use the PCs on the main floor for our real work. I like that." Brian said pointing to Filipe trying to give him some encouragement. Filipe merely bobbed his head in acknowledgement.

"We don't print anything unless we are forced to and if we do print anything, all previous versions of a document must be destroyed and once a document is no longer required it must be shredded then burnt. There has to be absolutely no paper trail." Brian paused again and began looking round for a shredding machine.

"No, we don't have one." Osvaldo said, anticipating Brian's next question. "I will bring one in tomorrow."

"Thank you Osvaldo." Brian replied. "One other thing, although I am jumping ahead a little here, on successful completion of the project, and it will be successful, we will immediately need to destroy the hard disks on all of the computers to destroy any evidence." Brian stopped again as Osvaldo explained the latest instruction.

"We could start formatting the disks as soon as the last transaction is made but it may be slow." José offered. Meanwhile Filipe was talking rapidly to Osvaldo and using his hand in a chopping motion. Then he held his arms out and smiled that huge grin of his. Osvaldo smiled too.

"Filipe is on top of it. He will extract every hard drive from the machines, smash them with an axe then throw them all into the river. Ten minutes tops and no technology would be able to extract any information from them." Osvaldo said quite proudly.

"Simple but effective." Brian said smiling. "I like it."

"Right. All that being said, I will start with a couple of activities that I know will have to be carried out," Brian stated as he walked to the flip chart. Now, just remember, for this session I just want to identify the activities. The how, when and who will be doing what we will decide at another session. First of all we will need the locations of all the ATMs in each city, how many are in each location and the bank they belong to." Brian began to write the task on the flip chart as he was talking. When he had finished he came up with the next task.

"We will need an ATM here in the building to carry out our testing." As Brian wrote that on the flip chart he asked Osvaldo if that would be a problem.

"No problem senor," he replied in Portuguese with a couple of expletives, "but its delivery will not happen quite as quickly as the shredder." At this the three men all burst out laughing and once it was translated to Brian, he joined in.

CHAPTER 11

Daily Routine

For the next few months Brian and Gracie fell into a comfortable routine. There was a small but adequately-equipped gym in the apartment building so typically, during the week, Brian would rise early and visit the gym. He would return to the apartment, shower, have breakfast and leave their apartment around 8:00 AM and return home at approximately 6:00 PM. Gracie would prepare dinner and they would dine together and discuss their days' events. Gracie meanwhile, would work out at the gym as soon as Brian left the apartment, then plan what she was going to do for the rest of the day. She had discovered a CANAM wives' club whose members were in Rio with their husbands who were there on postings. Of course, Gracie couldn't say she was with an embezzler seeking a safe haven. She would just explain her husband was a Project Manager on a hush hush banking project that he couldn't tell her very much about.

There were a couple of women Gracie had made friends with and she usually spent most of her days with them. One of the ladies had children attending an English-speaking school in Rio so they would get together once the children were dropped off. Sometimes Brian and Gracie would meet at social gatherings with the other couples. To date nobody had associated Brian with his escape, but nevertheless he was very nervous at some of the functions they attended as he felt it was merely a matter of time before his past was rumbled.

Usually at week-ends Brian and Gracie would just go to the beach or walk around the bohemian part of town trying out various restaurants and coffee shops. Once a month or during a long week-end they would take off to go camping. They had purchased a tent and all the essential equipment, sleeping gear, cooler, cooker and utensils. The equipment was permanently stored in the back of the SUV, so once they had purchased all their necessary vittles they could be out of the city and into the country. In addition to their camping gear they had purchased bicycles and a bike rack for the SUV. This gave them the freedom to ride around the vicinity of their camp site enjoying nature and the beautiful scenery that Brazil had to offer. On week-ends when they stayed in the city they would use the many bike lanes and trails to explore the city. The bicycles were permanently stored on their car and sometimes when Brian was at work he would often feel the need to get outside to take a break. One of his favorite ways of clearing his head would be to go for a bicycle ride beyond the line of decrepit buildings he was working around. He would reconnoiter the area within a ten mile radius checking out the local markets, stores and sights. Typically, he would do this early afternoon and on his return to the 'pits' he would have a quick shower, a bit of lunch prepared by Osvaldo and then refreshed, get back to work.

Occasionally Brian would have to work late or go the office the odd day on a week-end if things were not going quite to plan. He had created a work schedule and he was a stickler for ensuring all tasks were carried out on time. Each work day the team attended a huddle and Brian would put up a sign displaying in large numbers exactly how many days were left before the big day. Every day he would point out the total remaining days to each of the team and ask them whether they were going to hit their deadlines in a timely fashion. He didn't want to be in a position where he found out they were going to be late on the day of their deliverable so he insisted on knowing exactly how much effort was left for each task and if there were any risks that those dates were not going to be met.

To date, everyone on the team had responded well to the discipline and had not missed a single deliverable. But he also knew from experience the 'snowball effect'. They had an immovable deadline date and as it rolled closer and closer the deliverables would get tougher and tougher to achieve until corners had to be cut and quality began to get compromised. So it was imperative he keep on top of it and make sure the rest of the team responded accordingly. As a result, they rarely had to work late or on week-ends but there were those times where testing had to be carried out during off hours.

Osvaldo had gone one better than what Brian had asked for; he had requisitioned and installed two ATMs in the room. They had identified all the banks they would be hitting and they had downloaded the software that communicated with the ATMs from each of them. After some in-depth analysis and discussions with IT employees at various banks it all boiled down to three pieces of software that were integral to the whole ATM system.

To assist in the review of what they would be doing Brian had drawn a data flow diagram on the flip chart, highlighting the various software components integral to the project. He was of the opinion that a picture is worth a thousand words and with the added difficulties of translation issues he felt that pointing to the components as he mentioned them would be an asset. To help explain the overview he used a telescopic pointer to direct the team's attention to the various modules as he referred to them.

First there was the software on the ATM itself that communicated with the bank's host computer. The team established that they really didn't care too much about having to change the software for this aspect of the equation. Which was a great relief otherwise they would have to infiltrate thousands of machines in a short space of time on the day of the heist. However, the ATM software for each bank was customized and they needed a version for each of them for their testing purposes.

Secondly, there was the ATM Authentication software located on the bank's host computer. Once a card was entered into the ATM it triggered a communication with the ATM Authentication software on the host computer. As Diego Martinez correctly pointed out, this piece of software acted like a traffic cop. The code would direct control based on one of three things:

a. whether it was a banking card for their own bank
b. whether it was a banking card for an associate bank
c. the card was neither for their bank or an associate and/or it wasn't recognized

If it was a card for their own bank the software would direct the credentials to the third piece of the puzzle, the actual banking financial applications, to retrieve account details. The banking applications would then pass the information back to the Authentication software, which, in turn would send the data back to the ATM for display. After a successful transaction the banking applications, as a result of the ATM request from the client, would then update the appropriate bank accounts with the new balance. For an associate bank, information would be sent to their ATM Authentication system and would be processed in the same way.

Finally, for an invalid card no further action would be taken and a message would be sent back to the ATM accordingly. So basically each of the banks carried out the same processes, but there were no two pieces of software the same. However, for game day all they needed to hack and change was the ATM Authentication software for each bank. The new software would merely recognize the bogus card and send the appropriate signals to the ATM to have at it. But to ensure they fully understood the workings of each bank Brian insisted that they needed to simulate the way each of the banks currently worked so that they could replicate an ATM talking to every one of the banks the operatives would be hitting. There was plenty of time on the timeline to accomplish this and Brian felt it would be beneficial for troubleshooting purposes to fully understand and simulate how the current system operates.

So to accomplish this the first steps were to be in a position to download the appropriate copies of the software. They needed to obtain a copy of the ATM Authentication software for each of the banks that were going to get hit on game day. They also needed to be able to obtain copies of the appropriate ATM software each of the banks were using. José volunteered to make a call to his contacts and handle those tasks, he didn't consider that would be a problem. Finally for testing purposes, a stub needed to be developed that would simulate the bank's financial applications software that communicated with the ATM Authentication software. The stub would just be a small piece of software written just to fulfill the necessary communications in the absence of the real thing. Brian would be designated that task.

So, during the testing, a valid banking card of the bank owning the ATM would be entered into one of their two ATMs which had been loaded with the software for the appropriate bank, courtesy of one of José's contacts. The ATM software would then communicate with the ATM Authentication process for the same bank that had been loaded. This in turn would communicate with the stub, information and messages would be returned based on the responses to both the PINs and instructions entered on the keypad of the ATM. After successful testing this was then repeated with a valid banking card from an associate bank. Negative tests were also invoked ensuring that an invalid card was correctly rejected or a valid card from a bank that was not an associate was also rejected. After successful testing of one bank, software for the stub, ATM Authentication and ATMs were initialized and code for the next bank was loaded onto the computer and the ATMs. Then the whole process was repeated. On completion of testing for all the banks on their list, they were satisfied that their mock set-up was simulating the current banking system; they now had a benchmark. The next step was to modify the code to recognize the bogus card their operatives would be using while still being able to accept valid cards. Once this was achieved they would determine whether extracting and stashing cash from as many as ten machines, simultaneously, was a feasible proposition. For starters they would need a few custom-made banking cards and of course 200,000.00 REAL.

CHAPTER 12

The Party

One day Brian and Gracie received an invitation to a garden party hosted by one Diego Martinez. They had not met Martinez since that first encounter shortly after their arrival in Rio. They accepted the invitation and on the day of the party they arrived at the gates of Martinez's mansion in their Honda. Without any inspection by the security guards the gates opened and they were waved through to a parking area next to the helipad. From there, as they were that first time they were there, they were shuttled to the rear of the mansion in a golf cart, only this time it was a little less luxurious and it was being driven by one of a host of young men smartly clad in white jackets, black bow ties and black pants who had been employed purely to shuttle guests between the front of the mansion and the main party area.

As they turned the bend in the path at the rear of the mansion they were greeted by marquees covered in gaily-colored bunting, wandering minstrels and in the center, a stage with a group dressed in traditional Brazilian attire playing folk music. They were surprised by the sheer number of people in attendance. They were not exactly on time but they could hardly be considered late, yet the place was teeming with individuals. In the thick of things was Martinez, hobnobbing with his guests, unaccompanied this time by his adoring throng of semi-naked women. This was the first time Brian and Gracie had seen him standing and he was quite an imposing figure. He saw them, waved and began to walk towards them. He was wearing an immaculate, designer white suit with a white open-necked shirt. His short hair and mustache were perfectly groomed and his general appearance gave the impression of an extremely successful businessman, which in fact is what he was. His legitimate business dealings were as extensive as they were diverse. They included importing and exporting, a generic term covering a multitude of activities, which subsidized and concealed his illegal dealings. But that wasn't all. His fingers were in many pies: energy, transportation, shipping, amongst others. As a result he employed many people which provided him with a good platform to lobby politicians and other corporate bigwigs, many of whom were in attendance at to-day's party, an annual affair that was the highlight on the calendar for many of them. This year's theme was slightly different; it was a celebration of the games that Brazil would be hosting later in the year. Specifically a thank you to all the people who were responsible for bringing the games to Rio and the organizers who were working so hard to make it a success.

'If only they knew,' Brian thought.

"Ah, Brian, Gracie, so glad you could attend." Martinez said with genuine warmness giving Gracie a kiss on her cheek and an embrace. Brian thought the kiss lingered a little longer than etiquette suggested and his hands were a little too low for a casual greeting. But then Martinez was shaking his hand and speaking again and the thought was gone.

"Come, let me introduce you to some people and show you some of the culinary specialties that my chef has prepared." Martinez said eagerly. Before long, Brian and Gracie were rubbing shoulders with local rock stars, T.V. celebrities, and film stars. They were ushered along tables containing soups, hot and cold, salads, pizzas, meats, and all kinds of exotic fruits and vegetables. The dessert table was to die for and they ended up gorging on some of the finest food they had ever tasted. To whet their whistle there were drinks of all kinds, both alcoholic and non-alcoholic, but the best of all was the national cocktail of Brazil, the Caipirinha. Typically, this drink is made of cachaça, a type of rum made from sugar cane, half of a lime and two teaspoons of white sugar. But to add a little zest to the proceedings Martinez had organized a competition amongst the bar stewards as to who could concoct the best tasting Caipirinha. The winner was to be decided by the guests. Guests who tried the various drinks placed their votes in a ballot box. The entries would then be counted and the winner announced by Martinez later in the evening. Variations in the drinks were quite extensive, to a point that some purists couldn't call them a Caipirinha. In fact some of the competitors even substituted rum for the vodka and used various fresh fruits instead of lime. But that didn't detract from the fun or the delicious taste of the drinks, both Brian and Gracie enjoying their share, drinking their way through the different variations.

Brian even saw Filipe, José and Osvaldo there with their spouses and when Gracie was introduced to them she was finally able to put faces to the names Brian had spoken about while he was at 'work'. Because as far as Gracie was concerned, that was exactly what Brian was doing all day, working for Martinez in a legitimate business; no more criminal activity for him. This was confirmed shortly after the winner of the Caipirinha competition was announced when the contestant was awarded 5,000 REALs in cash. Brian and Gracie managed to catch the eye of Martinez to indicate they were leaving. He approached them and again thanked them for coming and realizing that they were both a little worse for wear after drinking maybe one too many Caipirinhas, he insisted they take a taxi home.

"The shuttle will take you to a cab." Martinez said.

"But I don't have enough cash on me for a cab ride home," Brian replied.

"Don't worry, it's all taken care of and don't worry about your car, it will be returned to you by the morning." Martinez said.

"That's very good of you Mr. Martinez." Gracie called out as she ungracefully climbed into the golf cart.

"My pleasure." Martinez said, smiling as he watched her almost erotic movements twisting and writhing onto the cart. Martinez turned to Brian and whispered, "how much does she know of your whereabouts during the day?"

"She doesn't," Brian replied, "she thinks I'm just doing a temporary job for you, like a contract."

"Excellent, so she has no idea of what you are really doing." Martinez smiled, "so things are going well and on schedule?"

"Absolutely, we have installed an ATM and successfully carried out testing. Our next step is the real thing, using a bogus card to clean the ATM out of all of its money. Just like you asked Diego." Brian whispered conspiratively.

"Ssh Brian, too many important people around," Martinez instructed as he put a finger to his lips, then he bade them farewell. This little conversation confirmed exactly the feedback he was receiving from the tails that were following them all over the city, the listeners to the bugs in their apartment and of course his man in the field, José.

CHAPTER 13

Some Snags

The team in the command post encountered their first real problem during their inaugural successful run with the bogus bank card and a full ATM. From a software point of view, everything proceeded like clockwork. The problem was the ATM, which could only dispense a maximum of 1,000 REALs at a time. So assuming there would be as much as 200,000 REALs in the machine, the operative would have to wait for 200 iterations for the ATM to empty, despite the machine being programmed to empty its hopper. This was a serious problem in terms of time if an operative wanted to hit as many as ten ATMs at a location before moving on to the next site. The team estimated that each dispensation of cash would take 10 seconds. Extrapolating that out would mean a full ATM would take at least 35 minutes to exhaust its funds from start to finish. Almost four times the estimate of ten minutes that Martinez had originally forecast. Furthermore, there was the problem of the money. The operative couldn't be expected to run from ATM to ATM gathering the money as it was dispensed as though it was some sort of contest on a T.V. game show. This had to be thought through before they could continue.

In the meeting room they began to brainstorm. "Right, here is what we could do and let's not think of reasons for and against at this point. That we can do later." Brian said. "Now, I'll start. We could add more operatives to the mix to hit more ATMs." Brian wrote that bullet point on the white board.

"We could extend the cut off time." Osvaldo offered, Brian responded by adding that point to the board.

"We could do both," José added. "The operatives could also start earlier," in response Brian added that point to the board.

"We could add extra operatives to work in tandem, shuttling one another to each location." Filipe suggested. That was also added to the board.

After much deliberation and a carafe of strong Brazilian coffee they had agreed on a scenario. Research would need to be carried out to determine all the high volume banks, i.e. the banks with the most ATMs at given locations. Some further assessment need to be undertaken if they couldn't find enough locations with at least ten ATMs. That would mean further relays to hit enough machines to reach their target. Once that was realized zones would then be determined and assigned to a tandem of operatives. They all agreed that was a job to be assigned to Deluca, who could initially find the resources to map out the ATMs and provide the operatives. The operatives would work in tandem, a driver and a passenger. At 2:45 on game day, or earlier if the coast was clear, the passenger would be dropped off at a location and the driver would continue to the next location. The passenger would ensure the bank was empty, then depending on the type of building the location was in, a sign would be displayed indicating the ATMs were undergoing maintenance. The location could be open-plan as in some of the bigger buildings, in which case the sign would be on a pedestal. If it was in a smaller location the sign would be taped to the door and either a wooden wedge would be placed under the door to prevent anyone else entering or a chain would be locked around the door handles, depending on the type of doors and which way they opened. Again, this would all be part of the reconnoitering to be carried out by Deluca's people. Meanwhile, the driver would repeat the process at the next location, and when he had finished emptying the ATMs he would return for the passenger and they would continue together to the next location assigned to their zone. If all went well it would take approximately two hours from start to finish to hit a minimum of thirty machines, maybe a little longer if there were insufficient high-volume ATMs in one location. They may be able to hit some additional singletons on the way back to the drop-off point.

They felt that the start time could be brought forward to 2:45 and in some of the locations earlier than that if the code could be uploaded and the bank was clear. Most of the operatives would then be finished around 4:45, with a few stragglers a little later. Neither proposed times were expected to create a problem. Most people would like to be seated around a T.V. at least fifteen minutes before kick-off time. It was also extremely unlikely the game would finish prior to 4:45. So driving to the drop-off points anytime up until 5:00 should still be traffic-free.

So by their calculations that would result in each tandem hitting 30 ATMs, and each ATM should contain up to 200,000 REAL. With 350 tandems in the field and the current exchange rate that would still net the target half a billion U.S. dollars. Even allowing for the extra expenses for the additional operatives.

They all sat back and digested that data. They double and triple-checked their figures but not only were they correct, they felt the plan was feasible.

Brian felt that the introduction of more operatives would, for sure, increase the risk of failure in terms of capture or informants and he said as much, "with all these extra operatives, isn't there a risk of someone informing the police?"

"Don't worry. Anyone who tries to sell Diego Martinez down the river will find themselves in the river." Osvaldo replied and the others all laughed. With that, Brian got the meeting back on track and the brainstorming continued.

It would require some training and trial runs for the operatives prior to game day but it appeared straightforward. There just remained the problem of the cash-gathering as it was dispensed from the machines. But Osvaldo had a solution for that. Each operative would be provided with large paper lunch bags. For each transaction duct tape would be added to one side of the bag and stuck to the ATM underneath the dispensing slot. The top of the bag would be fluffed open so the money would merely fall into the lunch bag, much like a horse and its nose bag. On completion of the transaction the bag and tape could be easily ripped off the ATM in one swipe and the packages dumped into a sports bag, not forgetting to remove the banking cards from the slots of course.

Further discussions were had and they all felt it was important for the operatives to assess their zone, check out their target branches and practice their routes for optimum timings. Prior to game day they must ensure they each have at least fifteen bank cards, a roll of duct tape, twenty lunch bags, a maintenance sign, and door-locking equipment appropriate to their targets. One more thing: the operatives must wear latex gloves at all times. Some of the operatives were known to the authorities and had criminal records, so leaving their fingerprints behind may not be the best of ideas. The operatives must all practice putting up the sign, securing the area, entering the card into the machine then positioning the lunch bag before moving on to the next machine and repeating the process. Then return to the first ATM to check that the money was flowing as it should then of course the subsequent machines. The last thing that must be carried out is the destruction of all their nefarious accouterments. This included the maintenance sign, the door locks, the banking cards, the disposal of the paper bags and the gloves. If possible, the items should not all be dumped in the same place. As they are driving to the drop-off point the passenger in the tandem will completely destroy all the bank cards by cutting them up into tiny unrecognizable pieces before throwing them down a sewer. The remainder of the stuff they could dispose of by any means possible but must not be near either the drop-off points or the banks that they had stolen from.

"Training," Brian said, "we will not have enough time to train all the operatives in the remaining time available. So I think we need to set up 'train the trainer' sessions. To do that we will need eight more ATMs to be installed here with full hoppers," Brian said, beginning to think this project was snow-balling. "Mr. Martinez would have to decide who the trainers would be for the cities outside of Rio and the arrangements for them getting here but we could handle one member of all the Rio tandems." Brian paused and walked around the table where the others were seated. "I think that covers everything. So, who would like to inform Mr. Martinez that if he wants his equivalent of half a billion U.S. dollars we will now need 700 operatives, eight more ATMs and 1.6 million REALs? Oh, and let's not forget the lunch bags."

CHAPTER 14

Toeing the Line

It was this request that forced a meeting between Martinez and José. José had discussed the details of the requirements with Deluca but once this information was passed on to Martinez he became skeptical. A meeting was arranged and Deluca drove with José to Martinez's mansion. The trip almost mirrored that of Brian and Gracie's, in that they were greeted by Eduardo and driven to the back of the mansion where they met with Martinez.

"Good day José, how goes the battle?" Martinez asked casually. He was trying to create a relaxed atmosphere but when you are summoned to the court of such a dangerous man the last thing you can feel is relaxed.

"It goes very well Mr. Martinez." José replied nervously.

"Any refreshments before we start?" Martinez asked.

"No, thank you Mr. Martinez." José replied.

"Now, David tells me that Beasley has asked for a whole slew of additional resources and money. Is that correct?" Martinez asked.

"That is indeed correct sir." José replied.

"In your opinion José, do you think these extraordinary resources are justified?" Martinez asked.

"Because of the problem with the ATMs, sir –" José began to reply but was interrupted by Martinez.

"Problem? What problem?" Martinez stopped eating a small sandwich and asked with a look of surprise.

"There is a limitation on the ATM in that it can only deliver a maximum of 1,000 REALs at a time. That is an issue we have had to somehow bypass. It's a mechanical limitation, not something we can control with software. But we figured if we could add more operatives, get them to work in tandem and stretch the time window the targets are still possible. But to test the feasibility of the exercise we would need up to 10 ATMs to practice on." José continued to explain and then reiterated the methods they were adopting and the need for training. When he had finished Martinez just stared at his small lake for a short time. Nobody else spoke. Without turning his head away from the lake Martinez continued. "So, José do you agree with Beasley? Is this the correct approach?"

"I believe it is sir." José replied. "Between us we beat this problem to death and it seems the only plausible solution." Martinez merely exhaled a little "Hmmm" and thought some more.

"What about the code changes? Obviously you have worked with Beasley on the programming-g. Anything to report there?" Martinez asked.

"He's good sir. Very good. I verify his code, not behind his back, he wants me to verify the code to ensure it is going to work. So far sir, I can't fault his approach or his work." José said with some pride in what they were achieving.

"Good to hear José, good to hear. After all José you stand to earn a great deal of money from this little caper, if you do as you are told." Martinez said pleasantly. But then his mood changed, he leant forward and looked straight into José's eyes. With a malevolent voice he said, "but let me tell you this José. I want you to keep a close eye on Beasley and the money. This money that has been requested is a fair chunk of change and enough to do a runner for in its own right. Do you understand?"

"Absolutely sir." José replied. If he was nervous earlier he was now almost quaking in his boots and a small bead of sweat appeared on both his brow and his top lip. It was just the effect Martinez wanted so he leant back and returning to his more pleasant voice he said,

"I will authorize this request and get David working on the additional resources for you." Martinez then looked away and reached for another small sandwich. The meeting was over.

CHAPTER 15

A Test Run

Every morning during the months leading up to game day Brian would update the 'Days Remaining' sheet, print it and tape it to the white board. At the end of the day's huddle he would ask each of the other men whether they were on schedule or had any issues. He would always end the conversation with, 'because you know we only have this many days remaining,' and point to the sheet taped to the wall. It became the subject of daily humor as the others usually joined in with the mantra.

Things were going very well in fact. The research had been carried out regarding the ATM sites and tandems had been tweaked to obtain optimum withdrawal with the tandems available. Deluca had recruited the operatives then supplied Osvaldo and Filipe with contact information. They worked with Deluca to schedule the operative training and on most days there were groups of Martinez's men simulating the tasks they would be performing on game day. The men were generally a motley crew of humanity, some of whom you definitely would not like to meet in a dark alley. Brian was very suspicious of them and made sure Osvaldo and Filipe kept a close watch on the money as it was dispensed by the ATMs during the practice sessions. In preparation for the training, which really could have been considered as dress rehearsals, Osvaldo and Filipe had put together kits containing all the paraphernalia necessary for the heist on game day. The kits were used during training to ensure the contents were correct and contained all the appropriate objects.

On those days that in-house training was occurring Brian and José would use one of the offices to review the code changes, desk check all their updates and prepare for a test to upload their changes into an actual bank. José was constantly asking questions about the methods Brian was using. Brian thought this was to learn exactly what and how he was facilitating the changes and didn't really show any concern. The fact was that they were now approaching the critical phase of their testing it made sense that José was backup in the event that something unforeseen happened to Brian.

Up until now they had successfully tested their software using the stubs that simulated the banks. Now it was time for the real thing, to hack into a bank and upload the software to recognize the bogus banking cards. After much deliberation it was agreed that they would select a bank with a branch across town so that there was little or no chance of anyone recognizing the person carrying out the test. Filipe, was chosen to make the withdrawal mainly because he was the least innocuous fellow of the group and was the most street-smart. He would be able to talk his way out of any situation in the event of any issues arising. The plan was for José to call Filipe on his cell to let him know when the hack had been uploaded and they were ready for the transaction. Filipe would make the first transaction by using his legitimate banking card to make a withdrawal of a thousand REALs. Assuming that was successful he would put in the bogus card and wait for the results. Hopefully, the ATM would begin dispensing until its hopper was exhausted.

The main issue was the timing of the test. If it happened during off-hours the banks would notice the money would be missing and would raise a red flag. After serious consideration it was decided that it should occur during regular business hours. Filipe would call the command post as soon as he had entered his bogus card and on the second iteration of one thousand REALs being dispensed he would just confirm the O.K. to Brian, hang up and shout out for help from one of the bank's staff. Meanwhile, Brian would back out the code update, remove all evidence of any transactions so that on investigation the only audit trail the bank's IT people would find was the legitimate withdrawal Filipe made, which was the removal of one thousand REALs from his account. Filipe would be standing there, feigning panic, in one hand he would have 1,000 REAL, his legitimate banking card and the transaction receipt while with the other hand he would try and keep up with the money pouring out of the machine. Filipe would also, surreptitiously, be timing the iterations to verify their calculations and he wouldn't be going anywhere until the last REAL came out of the machine so that he could confirm the start to finish time. Finally, as the bogus banking card was emitted from the machine on termination of the transaction Filipe would use sleight of hand, something he was adept at from his younger days on the streets of Rio, to switch the card to reveal his legitimate banking card.

This is in fact is exactly how it went down, except instead of feeling the panic he was demonstrating, inside he was as cool as a cucumber and the bank manager could not have been more grateful for Filipe's honesty. The bank manager on the other hand was feeling the complete opposite, outside he was trying to remain calm but he was in a state of panic and didn't quite know what to do. From nowhere Filipe had produced a lunch bag to collect the money and between the dispensations of the ATM, he emptied its contents into a bigger bag that one of the bank tellers had provided. Mercifully, the ATM finally spewed out its last note and the manager was so appreciative of Filipe and his ingenuity he gave him a gift card for a local restaurant pre-paid with quite a generous amount. Filipe used the card to buy a celebration lunch for the team one Friday afternoon, a couple of weeks before game day.

The bank's IT troubleshooting team investigated the incident and concluded that they couldn't find anything wrong with the bank's software. The audit trail showed the last transaction, Filipe's withdrawal, correctly listed and they could only assume there had been a malfunction with the hardware on the ATM which was subsequently replaced and returned to the manufacturer for service. Because Filipe, graciously, never left the bank and the fact that all the money was recovered there was never a hint of any intent of foul play. Therefore there had been no need for the IT personnel or the manager to follow up with any details of the account that had been used during the legitimate withdrawal. If they had done they would have discovered it was owned by a non-existent individual residing at a non-existent address.

CHAPTER 16

A Grisly Occurrence

One particular day things had not been going as well as Brian would have liked and he decided to stay behind after normal business hours to fathom out some coding issues. José volunteered to stay behind to assist him but Brian insisted he would be better off left alone. Osvaldo was also willing to stay late but they compromised. Osvaldo cooked him up a three course meal that was suitable for re-heating and he left it in the microwave for Brian to heat up whenever he wanted it. He called Gracie to let her know he would be late home and not to wait up for him and yes he would be eating dinner at the office. Not long after he had finished talking with Gracie he had to go upstairs to use the facilities. As was his wont when working late the desk light, the lights from the computer screens and any light streaming in through the building's windows were usually sufficient for his needs. As he was making his way downstairs he heard the crunching of gravel being made by a car pulling up outside the adjoining building. He turned and went quietly back up the stairs and walked along the gantry to look out of the small front window. All he could see was Deluca's limo outside. Nothing happened for a few seconds then both front doors opened simultaneously and out stepped Deluca and the brute of a man that was his driver. Without hesitation the driver opened the rear door of the car and lunged into the passenger area to haul out a small man who was screaming all sorts of pleas in Portuguese. Deluca had unlocked the large door of the adjoining building and the small man, who was still mouthing all sorts of what sounded like prayers, was dragged effortlessly into the building by the behemoth. Once they were inside and the doors closed Brian quietly went downstairs to the command post in an attempt to hear what was going on next door. Apart from the odd word he couldn't hear exactly what was being said but it was definitely an interrogation and the questions were not emanating from the little man. Every so often Brian would hear a slap or a punch and the man would scream out in pain still praying for mercy. So obviously he had perpetrated some wrong doing against them or Diego Martinez but exactly what Brian couldn't fathom. After about thirty minutes of questioning there was a pause in the proceedings where nothing was said and no movements were heard. Suddenly, Brian heard a high-pitched scream come from the man which sounded like "Nooooo", then a brief noise like a 'phut' that could have been a gun shot, then nothing.

Shortly after that there was the noise of something being dragged along the ground towards the rear of the building and the sound of a door being opened. Brian quietly walked toward the back of the room to try and optimize the sounds coming from next door. For a short time he heard nothing, then there was a splash as if something had been thrown into the river. The rear door was then closed and Brian heard steps that sounded like two people walking to the front door. Brian heard the front door being opened and closed then he heard rather than saw two car doors being opened and closed; the car started and with a spray of gravel it took off and was gone. By now, Brian was huddled, hidden behind one of the ATMs just in case Deluca or his driver decided to check on the command post. Brian felt sick with fear. He was sweating profusely and was truly terrified. He didn't understand, how they didn't see his car parked outside he'd never know. Or maybe they did and they just didn't care. As he was sitting there he recalled Osvaldo's remark during one of their brainstorming meetings, "anyone who tries to sell Diego Martinez down the river will find themselves in the river."

"What the hell have I got myself into?" Brian whispered to no one there.

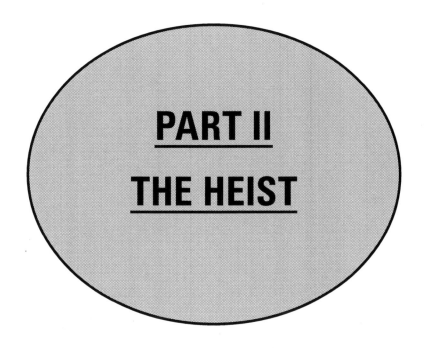

PART II
THE HEIST

CHAPTER 17

Game On

They were now into the final phase of the project. Brian was busy writing computer procedures so that their revised code could be uploaded to the banks' systems automatically. With the automated procedures written all the updates could be made to the banks simultaneously. This would occur during the morning of game day. This would provide them with some leeway to fix any glitches that might arise, not that they were expecting any. The ATMs could still be freely accessed by legitimate banking cards so no one would be any the wiser of the hack.

Before they knew it, game day arrived. Brian was at the command post at 8:30 and was still the last to arrive. The first thing he did was to print the 'Days Remaining' sheet and pin it to the white board only to-day, instead of pronouncing his usual mantra he merely said "if we're not ready by now we've had it." This got everyone laughing and released some of the tension that was beginning to build. Osvaldo had already prepared the coffee and laid out pastries, doughnuts and muffins on the meeting room table. José had started to write all the tasks that had to be carried out on the white board in the order they had to be actioned. He was working from a cheat sheet that had been printed from a secure PC. The cheat sheet reflected the play list that they had been honing for the last couple of weeks. They were satisfied all scenarios and contingencies had been mitigated. By 10:00 AM they were happy that the white board reflected their lists, so they shredded their cheat sheets and Osvaldo went to work with his axe on the disk drives of all the PCs that were no longer required. While Osvaldo was taking the remnants of the drives to the river José wiped that task off the board.

At 10:15 AM the owner of the fruit and vegetable business who delivered produce to Diego Martinez's mansion on a daily basis arrived in his large truck. He was closely followed by his son driving a non-descript pick-up truck with no logos anywhere on it. The owner turned off the ignition of his truck, got out then walked to the pick-up truck, got in and his son drove them away. José wiped another task off the white board.

By 11:00 AM Filipe had set up the configuration of the PCs as per Brian's instructions. There was a central computer that Brian would work with and use for troubleshooting if and when necessary. There were two computers on either side of the central computer so that Brian could monitor the withdrawals taking place in the four cities and they were labelled: Rio de Janeiro, Sao Paulo, Brasilia and Salvador. José wiped off another task from the white board.

Now they came to the moment of truth. Time to hack into all the banks and upload their code. Brian initiated the procedures and by 11:45 AM all the automated coded to make the necessary uploads were successfully completed. They looked in earnest at the four monitors and gradually figures started to appear on the screens. There was an entry, with figures, for all the banks they had hacked. They all jumped up with joy and gave each other high fives; this proved that the uploading of their code had been successful. At this time none of the bogus cards would have been utilized but the stats that were being displayed could only have been reported by their software. José scrubbed another item off the list.

That meant there was little else for the team to do so Brian suggested they take the afternoon off and spend the rest of the day at home watching the game with their families and friends. That way if anything did go wrong and illegal activities were traced back to the command post there was nothing that could be pinned on them. Filipe and Osvaldo were delighted at the unexpected turn of events as they were huge football fans and couldn't wait to get home to watch the game with their friends and loved ones. José not so much; he lingered long after the others had left and questioned the fact that Brian would be working there on his own.

"I think there should be at least two of us, just in case." José insisted. But Brian was adamant. "This afternoon could get quite stressful and as you know, I work much better on my own, especially if things were to go awry. I would be the only one who could fix things in the short time frame we have available to us. Anyway, nothing is going to go wrong. Preparation is the key here and we, you and I," Brian said pointing first to José then to himself, "have thoroughly prepared for this day. No, you go home and relax. I've got this, really." Brian was convincing so in the end José gathered his things and reluctantly left the building.

Brian continued to monitor the transaction activities on his monitors. He could total amounts by ATM, location or bank for either bogus or legitimate bank cards. These statistics would be beneficial as they approached the cut-off time to understand exactly how many locations remained to be hit. At 1:55 PM the first bogus card showed up on the stats, a little earlier than expected but not necessarily a problem. The only worry was if a legitimate customer went to the bank after the operative had left and discovered there was no money in the machines the customer may phone the bank. The first thing they would do was check the transaction history for that particular machine. They would not find anything untoward so they would be forced to send out a technician to investigate: good luck with that one.

At 2:15 Deluca and his man drove up to the command post. He was preparing to visit each of the call centers to monitor progress. But first he wanted to check in with Brian to ensure everything was going as planned. The first thing he noticed was the absence of the rest of the team.

"Where is the rest of your team Brian?" Deluca asked quite concerned.

"Oh I sent them home." Brian replied waving it off with his hand. "Everything is under control and like I told them, if anything was to go wrong I work better on my own."

"Even José?" Deluca said looking around as if José was going to appear out of thin air.

"Actually I think José secretly wanted to watch the game all along." Brian replied. Up until now Deluca's demeanor had always been casual, cool and in control but what Brian saw now was an angry, sullen Deluca as he turned on his heels and quickly went back to the car. No sooner was he in the car when the driver took off in a spray of gravel.

Some of the selected operatives had worked on synchronized thefts for Martinez on previous occasions and if they felt the timing was good then they knew best. Consequently, it wasn't long before stats from other locations began to appear, followed by those from the other cities. Before long the total had exceeded one million REALs and showed no sign of stopping. The figures began to flash quicker than he could follow with the naked eye and in no time they had hit ten million REALs. It reminded Brian of watching election results appearing on the T.V. as figures constantly changed as counted votes were coming in from the various constituencies. Brian decided to focus on his list of locations that were being hit, as the stats showed that the total number of ATMs for a given location had been exhausted he drew a line across that name on the list. Yet another piece of paper that had to be shredded on successful termination of the project.

Out in the field the operatives were, for the most part, sticking with the game plan. As expected, the streets and banks were deserted with just a few exceptions. Where there were too many people milling around the strike zones the operatives would move onto their next point of call and double back. In some cases the operatives were forced to wait until a customer left a bank, in others they just began to do their thing and politely but forcibly evict anyone in their way.

At 4:00 PM the total withdrawn using the bogus cards had reached 920 million REALs and no glitch had shown up or had been reported. By 5:00 PM there were just a splattering of their listed ATMs that either had not been hit or were not going to be but the grand total had hit two billion REALs. At 5:35 PM the first regional pickup van had arrived at the command post and ATMs were still getting hit. At 6:00 PM the second of the three vans arrived and by now the computer displays were showing the stats had peaked out at 2,100,000,000 REALs, give or take a few. At 6:30 PM the last of the vans arrived. The plan was for the drivers to transfer the bags that had been collected from their vans to the big grocery and vegetable truck parked outside the building. Once the transfer was complete one of the van drivers would drive the truck to Martinez's mansion and the other drivers, plus the spare driver, would take off in their respective vehicles. Meanwhile, Brian would shred and destroy any paper trail by burning the contents of the shredder in a steel drum conveniently located outside the building. He would wipe off the white board with isopropyl alcohol so that no trace of anything they had written could be detected and finally destroy the remaining hard drives à la Osvaldo's suggestion by axing them to pieces and then throwing them into the river. He had thought about creating procedures to back out all of the code he had uploaded but then realized it was superfluous. By then the banks would know they had been swindled, whether they could find the code or not. Finally, Brian would then turn off all the power at the mains, lock up and leave the command post forever. He would then drive away in his Honda and meet with the rest of the team at Martinez's the following day for a celebration.

Consequently, at 8:05 PM a truck bearing the logo Primo Fruit and Vegetable Company arrived at Martinez's mansion. The security guards were expecting it and the gates slowly opened. As the truck was driven up the driveway to the front of the house, bags were being unloaded by Martinez's henchmen from three helicopters that had landed on the helipad. Martinez had been made aware that the truck had entered the grounds and he had left the mansion and was strolling down the pathway to greet the truck, smiling broadly. Martinez was accompanied by two beautiful, bikini toting women, one attached to each of his arms and he was eager to show them the color of money, lots of money. But as the truck came to a stop in front of him he heard a shout of 'Riva, Riva, Riva' emanate from inside the truck and a squad from the BOPE team (the Special Police Operations Battalion of the Rio de Janeiro Military Police - Batalhão de Operações Policiais Especiais) jumped from doors on both the side and the back of the truck. This was accompanied by the sound of six armed military helicopters zooming over the grounds. Four of the helicopters were assigned to cover the mansion, one on each side and one of the others hovered over the helicopters parked on the helipad to prevent a hasty take-off. The sixth helicopter just circled in the event reinforcements were necessary. In addition, squad cars roared through the gates that had been secured by other members of the police force. Martinez's security guards were caught by complete surprise and were disarmed without a single shot being fired.

The smile had quickly faded from Martinez's face and the women that had been attached to his arms were now crouched on the ground desperately holding each other sobbing with fear. Martinez himself was just standing rigid as he faced the barrels of four rifles being aimed at his head by four experienced pros who knew how to use them. His face reflected the color of his white, tailored golf shirt as the blood drained from his face as one of the guards shouted,

"Diego Martinez you are under arrest."

CHAPTER 18

Busted

Lieutenant-colonel Manuel De Sousa of the Brazilian Federal Police Force arrived at the front of Martinez's mansion in one of the squad cars streaming through its gate. He was enjoying this moment as he had finally caught the great Diego Martinez red-handed; it would be interesting to see how the big man crawled his way out of this one. De Sousa waited for his chauffer to open the rear door of the squad card. De Sousa made a theatrical attempt at adjusting his perfectly pressed uniform and surveying the results of the raid before spinning on his heel and addressing Martinez.

"Well, well, well. Mr. Martinez it seems you have been very busy to-day. Watching the game was you?" De Sousa said sarcastically. He knew he would get no reply from Martinez, just that cold hard stare. Martinez was well aware of who he was facing, they had crossed swords many times in the past. But Martinez knew the drill: say nothing. He had been in this situation before, many times. De Sousa had an idea of what was going through Martinez's head but this time De Sousa was confident he finally had his antagonist at his mercy.

"Mr. Martinez. I think you will find things different this time. I have a warrant here to search your premises in relation to the theft of over two billion REALs. I have an accomplice who will testify against you. I have 700 of your operatives in custody. Oh, I also have the equivalent of a half of a billion dollars stashed on your properties which have been stolen from banks in cities all over the country. How does that grab you Mr. Diego Martinez?" De Sousa said smugly as he walked behind Martinez and began to read him his rights. "Now I wish to question you as my men carry out their search of your property but I will give you the decency of carrying out the initial interrogation in your home, unless of course you would prefer to join us at our humble police station?" De Sousa was getting cocky now as he spoke to Martinez but the big man merely turned on his heel to walk back to his house with De Sousa and a couple of his men in hot pursuit. The distraught women went running ahead of Martinez but they were of no concern to the authorities and they just let them proceed.

Martinez walked into the house, down a flight of stairs and into a spacious office. The Lieutenant-colonel and his two armed men followed Martinez into the office and they were surprised to see another man already seated there. The man rose out of respect for Martinez as he walked with some purpose to a chair on the far side of the room that obviously belonged to him. De Sousa's men raised their guns and pointed them at the man in the office. The man, totally unruffled by the armed police, was still standing when he said, "my name is Victor Monsanto. I am Mr. Martinez's lawyer."

"Good day Mr. Monsanto," De Sousa said, "we meet again." The men with the guns relaxed and De Sousa then ushered the two policemen out of the door to stand guard.

Monsanto was an older man, in his late sixties but his mind was sharp and Martinez had relied on him many a time to provide legal protection from the law. He was portly, of medium height with a full mop of grey hair that hung over a round clean-shaven face. He wore no spectacles as his eyesight was as keen as his intellect and Martinez trusted him implicitly. Monsanto sat down and said nothing, waiting for De Sousa to start the proceedings. De Sousa took off his cap and laid it on the large table that separated him from Martinez and his lawyer. When De Sousa sat down he realized that Martinez's side of the table was on a raised plinth so that he could look down on any guests that came into his office. An intimidation factor that De Sousa tried to shake off before he began speaking.

"We are about to throw the book at you Martinez. Embezzlement, grand theft, conspiring to defraud and that's just for starters -" Before De Sousa could continue Monsanto put a hand up and interrupted him.

"Mr. De Sousa, before you go any further, exactly what are you talking about? I have spent the entire afternoon here with Mr. Martinez watching the football match and all the festivities. What are these accusations all about?" Monsanto asked with great authority having been used to dealing with De Sousa and his ilk many times before in police stations and courtrooms.

"To-day a major crime has been perpetrated by men on Mr. Martinez's payroll under his instruction." Lieutenant-colonel De Sousa said in the typical police fashion portrayed in crime movies. "The crime was committed by his men," De Sousa emphasized by pointing at Martinez. "It was his men who stole over two billion REALs from ATMs across the country."

"That's a ridiculous charge to make," Monsanto replied. "Do you have the names of these men that you allege are on Mr. Martinez's payroll?"

"Oh yes, all approximately 700 of them," De Sousa said, "but of course you won't find them on any payroll."

"Then I fail to see how you can accuse Mr. Martinez of any wrongdoing if he has had no association with these men." Monsanto replied confidently.

"But I have a witness that can testify that these men were supplied by Mr. Martinez." De Sousa replied with a smirk.

"Has this witness personally met the alleged 700 men?" Monsanto asked.

"Some of them, not all." De Sousa replied. "But what about the money? These 700 men stole millions of REALs from banks and now we have all this stolen money found on Martinez's property. How do you explain that? Ha!" De Sousa said, quite proud of himself.

"What money?" Monsanto simply said.

"The money brought here by helicopters that landed here at the mansion and the money in the building they call the command post. Both properties owned by Mr. Martinez." De Sousa replied confidently.

"Of course he owns this house but again sir, what money and what property owned by Mr. Martinez are you referring to?" Monsanto replied.

"Don't play games with me Monsanto. Martinez knows perfectly well what money we are talking about." De Sousa shouted getting quite agitated now.

"I'm afraid he doesn't" Monsanto replied sounding confused. "The helicopters have nothing to do with Mr. Martinez. Why they landed here is something my client would also like to know as this is listed on the aeronautical charts as a private helipad. If the helicopters were, as you stated, hauling stolen money, how would my client possibly know anything about it if he doesn't know anything about the helicopters in the first place?" At this last remark De Sousa called in one of the guards.

"I want you to go to the helipad and interrogate the three helicopter pilots. Ask them why they landed here, get their flight plans that will tell us their original destination, ask them where did their cargo originate and who is picking it up at their final stop. Got that?" De Sousa ordered brusquely.

"Yes sir," replied the policeman and he was gone.

"Yes but you still haven't explained why money was taken to one of your properties. How do you explain that?" De Sousa continued.

"Yes, you have me stumped there," replied Monsanto, quite concerned. "However, Mr. Martinez owns lots of properties, condos, houses, factories, strip malls. Where exactly is the one you are referring to?"

"Next to the Guandu River just south of highway 493." De Sousa replied again oozing with confidence.

"Well I can assure you Mr. Martinez owns no property around there." Monsanto replied with equal confidence. "I have been with my client since he purchased his first property and I can say with all certainty that Mr. Martinez does not own any property in that area. As you know, I have lived here in Rio all my life, as I recall that area contains a number of derelict and deserted buildings. I'm afraid Mr. Martinez would not have any business aspirations in that part of the city."

"You can't fool me Mr. Monsanto. You think you are clever don't you?" De Sousa replied, although he was beginning to doubt the facts himself. "You know and I know that Mr. Martinez may not own those buildings but he financed the dealings for the people whose names are on the deeds."

"That is purely conjecture," Monsanto replied, "still not enough to charge my client with anything."

De Sousa still had one more trick up his sleeve and he was about to call it when the policeman returned with the statements from the three pilots. The policeman had duly asked the questions supplied by his superior and began to read ad verbatim from his notes.

"It materialized that the pilots had all filed flight plans crisscrossing the country that just happened to have Mr. Martinez's mansion close to their flight path. They had all, coincidently, encountered technical difficulties while in flight, which had been duly reported to the authorities on the emergency wavelength and it was suggested that because they were so close to Mr. Martinez's helipad it would be expedient to land to check out the mechanical fault. As for the cargo, none of the pilots had any idea who instigated the delivery or who it was destined for, they were merely cargo pilots and had nothing to do with the shipment details. The reason for the unloading of the cargo was to lighten the load of the helicopters as their instruments indicated the fault may have been caused by overloading." After the reading of his notes the policeman returned to his post outside the office door.

"What a convenient coincidence." De Sousa sneered. "They all just happen to land here carrying a pile of stolen money and Mr. Martinez knows absolutely nothing about it."

"Well I think that sums it up perfectly." Monsanto replied haughtily.

"Well what about the fruit and vegetable truck, hey?" De Sousa asked feeling that this was a clincher. "Why was your client so eager to meet the truck? In fact, what was it doing making a delivery at this time on a Saturday afternoon when I know for a fact deliveries arrive here only during the mornings?"

"It just so happened that my client was going for a walk around the grounds with a few of his guests when the truck came up the driveway. As you said Mr. De Sousa, the arrival of the truck was totally unexpected and the fact that my client was out there at the same time was pure coincidence." Mr. Monsanto said coolly as if it was obvious to everyone.

"Why the delivery was being made at such an irregular time is maybe a question you have to ask the owner of the truck."

"Don't you worry, I will." De Sousa replied and immediately called in one of his policemen again. "Find out the owner of the truck you came in on. Get in contact with him and ask who has been using his truck this afternoon. Do you remember the name of the company? The logo was on the side, 'Primo Fruit and Vegetable Company' I think it was."

"Yes sir." The policeman replied and went to make the necessary phone calls. He was gone around ten minutes while De Sousa continued to pump questions and Monsanto continued to skate around them while Martinez sat stoically staring at the lieutenant-colonel with those cold black eyes. On his return the policeman once again referred to his notebook and recited what he had written.

"The owner's name is Domingos Delgado and he has spent the whole day at home with his family preparing to watch the football match. When I asked him why his truck was at Mr. Martinez's mansion he replied that it must be a mistake. He had spoken to Mr. Martinez's chef on Thursday to see if he could make an extra delivery yesterday so that he didn't have to come all this way out here to-day when he had so much to do at home. The chef said, "no problem," so after his last delivery yesterday the truck had been locked up in his garage for the week-end. When I told him his truck was here he told one of his sons to go and check the garage. When his son returned he said that the garage had been broken into and the truck was gone. So I told him not to bother calling the police because it had already been found." The policeman finished, closed his notebook, put it back in his pocket and quickly left the room. He, like De Sousa, did not believe the interrogation was going in the favor of the good guys.

"Yes you might have an answer for everything right now but with my witness's testimony you're going down." De Sousa snarled though his bared teeth but it certainly didn't faze Monsanto.

"Well that's just it Mr. De Sousa, you keep mentioning this witness person and his or her complicity in the theft but who exactly is he or her and where is his or her statement?" Monsanto asked. De Sousa smiled and waited for a few seconds before replying.

"It's a he Mr. Monsanto and he will be here presently with a statement containing enough hard evidence to put you away for a very long time Mr. Martinez." De Sousa said looking first at Monsanto and then Martinez. He paused again knowing that he now had their full attention. "It's Beasley, Mr. Brian Beasley."

CHAPTER 19

A New Realization

At the sound of Beasley's name being mentioned, Martinez's face turned crimson with rage, his fists were clenched and he was coiled as taut as a spring ready to tear apart the man who was named as the witness, even so, Martinez remained tight lipped.

"Brian Beasley? Beasley? I can't say I recognize the name, has Mr. Martinez ever met the man?" Monsanto asked.

"Oh yes, he certainly has." De Sousa replied. "The first time Mr. Martinez had met our witness he had been kidnapped with his partner and brought here to this mansion against their will." De Sousa was beginning to raise his voice now for effect. "The second time was for one of Mr. Martinez's garden parties where they briefly exchanged a progress report of how the software changes were going for the hacking of banks to facilitate this robbery." At this statement Martinez gave a look of surprise while De Sousa smiled at him, "we have the conversation on tape Mr. Martinez. Mr. Beasley was wearing a wire." De Sousa sat back while Monsanto and Martinez whispered briefly for a few moments before Monsanto replied.

"Well as for their so-called kidnapping, my understanding is that Mr. Beasley was driven here to be introduced to my client to discuss current affairs. At the same time Mr. Beasley's partner was provided with a tour of the gardens by our head grounds man. We have video footage showing the delighted young lady smiling and waving to my client and Mr. Beasley. For someone who was kidnapped that is hardly a scenario one could consider. Furthermore, if, as you say they were kidnapped why on earth would they respond to an invitation to return?" Monsanto paused and looked inquiringly at De Sousa. "As for the recording you mentioned I don't believe Mr. Martinez has ever given you permission to record his voice, as a result, I'm afraid that evidence would be inadmissible in a court of law. I recall Mr. Beasley now and he was 'wired' alright. If I remember correctly, he and his partner consumed a high number of Mr. Martinez's specialty drinks, the Caipirinha that night. We have video evidence to prove it. Consequently the statement of someone who was as inebriated as Mr. Beasley and his partner could hardly be considered credible. In fact, Mr. Martinez provided a taxi to get them home and then arranged for their car to be driven to their apartment building. So forgive us if our views of the episodes you cite do not match yours." Monsanto stopped talking; the ball was back in De Sousa's court but he remained unflustered."

"Don't worry, the whole plan and the money are now in our hands and with Beasley's testimony with all the facts, places and names we will have enough evidence to charge you." De Sousa proudly stated.

"Well," Monsanto started to say, "his statement better be good because everything you have provided up until now is purely circumstantial without an iota of proof that my client is guilty of anything. Furthermore, from what you have told us during this interview it would suggest to any impartial observer that Mr. Beasley, with his known criminal record, that there is a whole stack of evidence that points to him as the perpetrator of this crime and absolutely none which can be attributed to my client," Monsanto offered eloquently in his courtroom voice. "So unless you can produce a cast-iron testimony I'm afraid this interview is terminated."

For the third time during the interrogation De Sousa called in the policeman from outside the door. Without turning his head he smiled and merely said, "bring Beasley to me." While they waited Martinez continued to sit motionless staring straight ahead at the wall as De Sousa had now risen from his chair and began to pace the room. Monsanto meanwhile shuffled a few papers and made a few notes on a notepad. It was a good twenty minutes before the policeman came back into the room, without Beasley.

"We can't find him sir." The policeman said sheepishly.

"What do you mean you can't find him?" An exasperated De Sousa replied, "where the hell did he go?"

"Apparently he was last seen driving the truck through the gates sir," the policeman mumbled.

"Driving the truck through the gates? What the hell did he do that for?" De Sousa asked.

"Don't know sir." The policeman was decidedly uncomfortable as he continued. "But there's something else sir. The money from the three helicopters had been loaded into the back of the truck before he left."

CHAPTER 20

Reality Check

"Get Beasley on the radio and tell him to get his ass back here immediately." De Sousa barked the order to the cowering policeman. The policeman left and came back a short time later.

"Apparently Beasley was not issued with a radio sir," the policemen quietly informed his boss.

"Then send a couple of squad cars to pick him up," an even more exasperated De Sousa shouted at the policeman. "He has obviously returned to the command post." De Sousa was now shouting his orders even louder with spittle spraying from his mouth as he did so. In his mind's eye this interview should have been a slam-dunk but things were not going as he had anticipated, what's more, his blood pressure was beginning to rise. Seizing on the opportunity Monsanto piped in, "well, I don't think there is much point in us staying here Mr. De Sousa. Perhaps you can inform us when your men have finished their search of the house and are about to leave the premises. We will be in the dining room; you know where that is. Good evening." Without hesitation both Martinez and Monsanto stood up and proceeded to leave the room and De Sousa felt a sense of helplessness. This whole operation had cost a fortune and it was on the verge of total failure. He did not have a shred of evidence to charge Martinez unless he could get Beasley's testimony and with him unaccounted for he was beginning to have a very bad feeling about this whole mess. To make matters worse the squad cars were having difficulties negotiating through the busy traffic to the command post, even with their sirens blaring out their presence. Rio de Janeiro is world-famous for its traffic congestion and with most of the city now coming out of their afternoon's hibernation after the football match it made matters even worse. Eventually, the squad cars made it to the command post and they reported back to their boss that the truck had not arrived but the vehicles used for the three pick up points were still locked up in the command post.

"Then he must have taken an alternate route in an attempt to avoid the traffic. Get back on the road and find him. I'll see if we can get those military helicopters in the air to help search." De Sousa told them and within seconds they were back within the mayhem that was Rio traffic, only this time it was infinitely worse as they were now going with the traffic as opposed to against it.

De Sousa managed to second two of the helicopters to assist in locating the truck but after a couple of hours and the traffic getting a little lighter there had been no sighting of the truck either by the squad cars or the helicopters. De Sousa decided to retrace their steps and return to the command post. Using a skeleton key he entered the building through the Judas gate just as Brian did all those months ago. Using a flashlight De Sousa located the main power switch and turned on the lights. The fluorescent lights flickered then began emitting a steady soft light to the whole room. De Sousa had a quick look around noting that whiteboards had been completely wiped clean, hard drives had been removed from the computers and were nowhere to be seen. Thankfully, the three vans were in the room but on closer inspection his worst fears were realized: the vans were devoid of any cash.

Quietly, De Sousa said to his next-in-command who was now standing by his side. "Send out an all-points bulletin to search for that fruit and vegetable truck. It can't have got far." Then more loudly so that all the others could hear, "check out the other buildings along here to see if Beasley is holed up in any of them. Hurry, hurry."

It didn't take long to realize there was no sign of Beasley or the truck in the immediate vicinity. So De Sousa shouted out more orders: "everyone back to the mansion and keep your eye on the road for that damn truck." He turned off the lights and locked the door. The squad cars roared down the road to the highway and as soon as they were out of sight a limo quietly turned onto the road and inconspicuously drove towards the command post with its lights off. It came to a stop just outside the command post and David Deluca got out of the car. Using a flashlight he unlocked the very same door De Sousa had used only a few moments ago. Deluca entered the building but didn't turn on the lights. With the use of his flashlight he looked inside the vans and noticed they were empty. Then he carefully made his way over to the bank of ATMs to check the contents of their hoppers. After checking the ATMs he left the command post then he and his driver carried out a cursory search of the other buildings. On completion they returned to the car to drive back to the mansion to report. Deluca now had three things to report back to Mr. Martinez. There was no money in the vans or the 10 ATMs, all 2.0 million REALs were missing from the hoppers, as was the Honda that Mr. Martinez had given to Brian.

CHAPTER 21

It's All Gone Wrong

In the aftermath of the theft full descriptions of Brian and Gracie were provided to all the national newspapers accompanied by recent photographs. Particulars of the truck with photographs were also published and a reward was offered for any information leading to the arrest of the two fugitives. The heist, one of the biggest in history, was front-page news not only in Brazil but around the world. It was receiving full attention by the major wire services, the T.V. stations as well as CNN and the BBC. The Brazilian authorities were also adding pressure to the police as the theft was beginning to overshadow the press coverage of the games.

As soon as the full realization as to the extent of the heist was made aware to the banks they were forced to shut down their systems temporarily. The hacked software that Brian had uploaded had to be overwritten with the banks' backup versions. Of course they also had to replenish the hoppers of all the ATMs with cash, which took considerably longer to fulfill than it did the operatives to empty them.

Meanwhile at the mansion Martinez passed the word to all of his men with an even higher incentive than the one offered by the police if they could bring him Beasley. As he told Deluca, "Beasley better hope that the police find him before I do." Martinez also had that extra piece of information that the police didn't have, the missing Honda and the tracking device that had been hidden underneath the rear wheel well. However, this proved to be a lost cause when the signal emitting from the device was located in a coal mountain in the northern part of the country after a wild goose chase by a pair of Martinez's henchmen. By now Martinez was beside himself with rage and everyone in his organization was avoiding him at all costs. So now there were two manhunts underway, one being carried out by the police and the other by Martinez's men.

Interrogations and investigations continued but nothing provided an inkling to the disappearance of the truck, cash or whereabouts of Gracie and Brian. It was as if they had just vaporized and melded with the atmosphere. The search by the police of the mansion yielded nothing, not even a hint of suspicious business dealings or other underhand activities. The ownership of the buildings that housed the command post was pursued and the police discovered they belonged to a young local resident who had purchased the deeds a year ago. After inquiries with friends and family none of them could understand why he had purchased the property. He had been diagnosed with terminal cancer and unfortunately, he died a few weeks ago. He was a bachelor and no connection could be found between him and Diego Martinez. The command post was stripped down as the police mined for evidence. The computer equipment and ATMs were taken away for forensic testing but the only fingerprints they were able to find were those belonging to Beasley, which they fully expected to find.

It got worse for De Sousa as it appeared that they would have to release all the operatives. There was just not enough evidence to charge them, even for a misdemeanor. On game day, as the operatives drove in to their respective checkpoints they were immediately apprehended. They were told by the arresting officers to get out of the car and toss the bags they had with them into a waiting van, the one that would later be driven to the command post with all the money. The operatives' hands were then immobilized with wrist restraints and they were led into a small hall where they were sat down to wait. One of the policemen then drove the car out of the building into the adjacent car park. The buildings were all similar, a large garage on the side where the occupants of the cars could exit in privacy and in this case also unload in privacy. Each building had a large room with chairs, tables and presentation equipment. After the first few operatives from each city had been interrogated, it materialized that their stories were identical and it was obvious that they had been well prepared. The police in each city swapped notes and reluctantly made the decision that there was no point continuing the interrogations with the remaining operatives as their stories would all be the same. As a result, without any evidence or the stolen money, they could not hold the operatives; and it was agreed that they should all be released. It was left to De Sousa to make the final decision to release the operatives but before he did he wanted to read a sample transcript from one of the first interviews:

Police:	Tell me in your own words what happened.
Operative:	I went to the bank machine to withdraw some cash.
Police:	How much?
Operative:	1,000 REAL
Police:	And what happened?
Operative:	I put in my banking card and withdrew 1,000 REAL from my bank account. Look I have the receipt.
Police:	Let the record show that a valid receipt has been shown. Then what happened?
Operative:	The machine went loco and began to spew out money. The bank was closed so all I could do was gather the money with the intention of returning to the bank on Monday to explain what happened.
Police:	So how do you explain turning up at a meeting point with tens of other men all carrying the same type of bag all full of money from ATMs that had gone loco?
Operative:	We were all attending the same football seminar. The total cost was 1,000 REAL but a deposit of 500 REAL had to be paid at least a week prior to the seminar. I went to pay the deposit which is when I was issued with a sports bag and some other gifts. On attendance at the seminar the balance had to be paid, which was the remaining 500 REAL. But I needed some additional cash so I went to the bank machine before attending the seminar and withdrew 1,000 REAL. I expect a lot of the other attendees had to do the same. How was I to know the machines would go haywire?

Police: But that doesn't explain why you tried every one of the other ATMs in the building.

Operative: I'm an honest man, I would hate to see the bank be out-of-pocket because of a machine malfunction. I had some time so I tried all the other machines. I couldn't just leave the money there - a thief may come and take it so I had to bring it with me.

Police: But when you arrived at the meeting point the car you were travelling in contained more than two sports bags, all full of money. How do you explain that?

Operative: I only saw two bags in the car I was in, one of which was mine. If as you say there were more than two bags then they must have belonged to the other guy in the car, you would have to ask him.

Police: And what was the other guy's name?

Operative: Don't know.

Police: Why don't you know the other guy's name?

Operative: Because of the national football match many of us were having difficulty obtaining transportation to the seminar. The organizers kindly arranged pick-up points and we would be recognized by the uniquely colored sports bags that had been issued to us.

Police: Would you recognize the other guy if you saw him again?

Operative: Don't think so.

Police: One other thing. To date, this match was the biggest national football match of the year. Why would you use this very afternoon to attend a football seminar?

Operative: My understanding is that most of the people attending the seminar had trouble with the original start time, because of the game. So the organizers agreed to record the game and attendees could just arrive when they could and get acquainted. At 5:00 PM the seminar would begin and the recording would be used as a basis to discuss tactics, strategies and ball-control techniques.

De Sousa had read enough; all the remaining transcripts were a slight variation of the same theme. The operatives had really been De Sousa's last hope in attempting to get some clues as to Beasley's whereabouts. De Sousa knew for a fact that the operatives were cleaning out the ATMs at each location but without the stolen money he couldn't provide evidence that there were more than two bags per car. The bank's records corroborated exactly what the operatives were all saying; they withdrew 1,000 REAL and the machine malfunctioned. You certainly couldn't contest the operatives' honesty in saying they were going to return the money; they were never given the opportunity. Both the money and the operatives were in police custody at the time the money was re-stolen. Reluctantly, he approved the release of all the operatives. On reflection, De Sousa felt maybe that was where he made a mistake, they should have let the operatives toss the bags into the van themselves before their arrest. Which would have demonstrated some collusion then their story would not have held true. Of course his biggest mistake was trusting Beasley, he should never have let Beasley persuade him to come along for the ride.

The scenario provided by the operatives had been a refinement made by the team at the command post as a result of Filipe's test at the bank. They persuaded Martinez to provide additional REAL for each of the operatives so that they could open an account and deposit as many 1,000 REAL into it that they would need based on how many ATMs they were expecting to hit. They would obtain a legitimate banking card that they would use prior to the first withdrawal for each ATM at an assigned location. This would provide a legitimate audit trail and also pay the operatives at the same time, even though it was pretty much guaranteed that they would also grease their palms with additional funds from the stash. At the same time they were destroying their bogus banking cards they would also empty the cash from the lunch bags into the sports bags then dispose of the lunch bags. Being found with the taped lunch bags would definitely have been something they would have difficulty explaining.

By the second week after the heist and with no sign of Beasley or the money, the news stories regarding the theft had been pushed to the inside pages and by the third week they were almost non-existent.

During the fourth week there was little or nothing at all in most papers with the exception of the police federation's announcement regarding the suspension of Lieutenant-colonel De Sousa while an inquiry was being inducted into his possible collusion with criminal elements regarding the recent theft. This was more due to the pressure of the banks who were currently out-of-pocket and were insisting on being compensated for their loss. They needed a scapegoat and De Sousa was it. After all, the banks had cooperated fully with the police in allowing this theft to proceed under the guarantee that any stolen money would be returned and with the added bonus of capturing a whole gang that had been the scourge of Brazil for many years. Exactly how much money was being targeted, the extent of the thefts and the fact that their software was being compromised had not been shared with them.

One evening, months since the heist, De Sousa was again regurgitating the events of that day for the nth time. De Sousa was at the end of his tether. His career was over and his plush carpet of life had been pulled unceremoniously from under his feet. His despair had driven him to drink and he knew the path he was on was a slippery slope downhill. He had seen too many of his compatriots become alcoholics only to die an early death. He decided he was better than that and he felt it was time to pull himself together. He knew what he had to do, consequently, it was with great reluctance and a huge slice of humble pie that he decided to arrange a meeting. As a result, one Saturday evening, under the cover of darkness, the deposed, discredited Lieutenant-colonel De Sousa arranged a meeting with Mr. Diego Martinez at his mansion.

CHAPTER 22

Gone Over To the Other Side

De Sousa was a man who had been in the twilight of a successful police career. He was in his early fifties and on the verge of retiring, but the events of the last few weeks had aged him considerably. He had hoped that the capture of Diego Martinez was to be his swan song. He could visualize years of speaking engagements and the seminar circuit providing him with a life of luxury for his retirement years. Although he was a handsome man he was a bachelor, married to the police force and never wishing to settle down with a good woman to live a life happily ever after. Very early in his life he realized he was probably asexual and that part of life's pleasures was just not for him.

So here he was driving towards the lair of the enemy, to talk with the very man he had sworn to bring to justice. Martinez was to De Sousa as Moriarty was to Sherlock Holmes. Although the years had mellowed both of them and a mutual respect had developed between them, despite De Sousa's latest attempt to convict Martinez. The man had been a thorn in De Sousa's side ever since his attendance at Police College and it had continued all the way through his career. They had crossed swords many times with Martinez always walking away the victor. Over the years De Sousa had even attended many of Martinez's organized functions in an attempt to identify the man's contacts and dealings. They had often chatted together but never about work. The impression that De Sousa had always perceived of Martinez was that he was, deep-down, a kind, gentle man. Someone who he could talk to as a friend.

As De Sousa arrived at the gates to the mansion and as they slowly opened he realized he was at the point of no return. Once he crossed the threshold of the gates in front of him, in all likelihood his career was truly over. But now he had a bigger enemy than Martinez, someone who had taken his career, his credibility, and it had been brought about in such a back-stabbing, malicious way that it had made De Sousa look a fool in the eyes of his family, friends and public. Even Martinez would never have stooped to the antics Beasley had used. Yes, over the years Martinez had found De Sousa's attempts to implicate him very amusing but he had never tried to publicly humiliate him. Martinez appreciated the fact that De Sousa was just trying to do his job and respected the man's efforts and even his successes when other felons were brought to justice.

De Sousa stayed resolute, although with heavy heart he drove through the gates and parked the car. Eduardo greeted De Sousa at the front of the mansion. Eduardo showed De Sousa down to the same office where the interrogation took place the day of the game. Naturally, Martinez was accompanied by Monsanto, but in addition, David Deluca was also in attendance. Deluca and De Sousa had met before so everyone cordially exchanged pleasantries before Deluca displayed the obligatory wand for detecting concealed recording or transmitting devices.

"If you wouldn't mind Manuel," Martinez asked.

"Not at all." De Sousa replied and stood, arms outstretched for the scan. On completion, Martinez asked, "can I get you anything Manuel, a drink? Food? Anything you want."

"You know, I could do with a whiskey if you don't mind, this is extremely difficult for me." De Sousa replied, "a bit of Dutch courage perhaps."

"I understand fully," Martinez replied sympathetically, not quite knowing exactly what was on De Sousa's mind that was going to be difficult, "but you have nothing to fear here, you are amongst friends." Now, De Sousa thought that might be a bit of a stretch, but he knew what Martinez meant. Martinez instructed Eduardo to cater to De

Sousa's request and when he returned with the drink Martinez dismissed both Deluca and Monsanto. Monsanto was hesitant to leave Martinez alone in a room with a senior policeman, albeit a suspended one, but Martinez merely gave the slightest incline of his head to indicate everything was fine and Monsanto followed Deluca out of the room.

"Now Manuel, what can I do for you? Asked Martinez.

"As you must know by now Diego, this whole heist was set up for the sole purpose of your capture." De Sousa began. Martinez nodded his head indicating to De Sousa that he had pretty much gleaned that much based on the way things unfolded during the day of the game. "We were aware of something going down during the games but we couldn't obtain any hard facts. Our informants had snippets of information but nothing we could hang our hat on." De Sousa paused and took a sip of the superbly aged scotch Martinez had supplied. A huge improvement on the gut-rot booze he had been drinking since his suspension. "We contacted Interpol and after mulling over the facts as we knew them it was felt we needed to bring in someone you would be hard pressed to ignore. Interpol searched their databases, a little like looking for an organ for a transplant operation: we needed a perfect match. After researching a few likely candidates it was agreed Beasley was the man." De Sousa took a drink at the mention of Beasley. "He was serving the first year of a ten-year sentence for embezzlement and as he was a young man and perfect for our needs. So we approached him to see if he would work with us for the duration of the games. In return, his sentence would be commuted. The proceeds from his crime had never been recovered and it was agreed that if he would assist us in this endeavor they would not be pursued and he would be able to keep them. The banks had been recompensed by the insurance companies and the insurance companies had raised their rates so they no longer cared.

Needless to say Beasley jumped at the opportunity. It was arranged that Brian would be detained in the Rotunda, a brand-new computer-controlled facility that was touted as being an inescapable bastion. None of the personnel, warden, prisoners or guards were aware of his pending escape that was being arranged as it was felt for security purposes that would be for the best. Everyone knew that your tentacles are far-reaching and we didn't want to take any chances. Obviously the RCMP had to assist him with a few pieces of information and documents. They conducted follow up interviews under the pretense they were following the money trail but were really updating him on the deal. They even supplied him with a partner, Detective Sergeant Gracie Brown of the Ontario Provincial Police. She contacted the prison warden under the guise of being a journalist wanting to write a story on the great embezzler. In fairness, had certain information and specially designed apps. not been installed on Beasley's tablet he may still be in the Rotunda to this day and we would not be having this conversation. Now, here we are, the rest is history. Beasley escaped, made it to Rio, he and Gracie got married, to people who had no idea of the monster they were creating. The wedding was announced and we were successful in that enough breadcrumbs had been distributed to entice you into bringing him on board for your endeavors." De Sousa stopped to have another swig of his drink.

"Congratulations Manuel. I must admit, I had no idea." Martinez said sincerely. "For once you had me completely fooled."

De Sousa acknowledged the compliment by raising his glass and taking another drink, "Thank you Diego. High praise indeed." De Sousa put the glass down and continued.

"We were certain that you would put tails on both Beasley and Gracie and we were certain their apartment would be bugged. We also suspected one of the team at the command post would be a mole but we never did find out who."

"It was José, but no information ever got passed to us that was of any use or indicated that this was a set-up." Martinez said, casually thinking that if they were going to share intelligence he would show some willingness and let out a small snippet of information. Then he added; "unfortunately, José had a little accident the day after the game. We don't know the details exactly but it appeared he got into an argument with some rival football supporters who accused him of taunting. Someone pulled a knife and, well, it was unfortunate." Martinez's voice trailed off.

"I wonder if Beasley knew José was spying on him. He probably did. I think we underestimated Beasley. He made sure nothing was communicated unless he wanted it to be; that's why José had nothing of importance to tell you." De Sousa added before continuing, "As you know Gracie joined the CANAM club. This had been planned and she made contact with a Debbie Tansley. Debbie had two young children and was the wife of a diplomat working at the U.S. embassy. Prior to her first pregnancy and her husband's posting to Rio she just happened to have been a detective in the Washington DC PD.

Anytime Brian needed to pass on any information he would write it down on small notes which were then given to Gracie to be left in Debbie's car after their day trips or shopping excursions. Nothing was ever spoken, so your listening devices were of no use to you and your surveillance guys would never have known messages were being passed. It all looked quite innocent. Debbie would then pass the information to her husband who would contact me, and only me, to relay the details."

"Again Manuel, I had no idea," said Martinez shaking his head in disbelief.

"I trust that what I am telling you will not encourage you to engage in repercussions on the Tansleys as they were only doing what they thought was right." De Sousa pleaded.

"Absolutely not Manuel. You have my word. All I am interested in now is Beasley and that broad of his." Martinez assured him. To most people, believing the word of an arch-criminal like Martinez may be as believable as being able to turn lead into gold. But for all of his shortcomings De Sousa thought of Martinez as a man of his word and De Sousa had no qualms about the Tansleys' safety.

"But your account of the events is very interesting; please continue." Martinez said. Before De Sousa could carry on, Eduardo appeared with a second glass of whiskey. De Sousa nodded his thanks, waited for Eduardo to depart and continued.

"So basically we knew everything that was going to take place: the truck, the helicopters, the drop-off points, locations, operatives everything. The only concern we had was the video cameras you had set up around the command post. We had to get a squad of police to the command post to position themselves in the truck instead of the cash you were expecting. The pickup vehicles would also be driven in by policemen, not your operatives. But Beasley had a solution for that.

We knew what time Delgado was delivering his truck, and once he was gone we would be clear to bring in a squad of police to travel to your mansion in the truck. Once Brian had dismissed Osvaldo, Filipe and José, he used the cell phone he said that you had given him at your very first meeting to make a call to the mansion. Brian knew it would be answered by the guy in your control center who would have to leave the room to find either you or someone else to find you. Brian took that opportunity to hack into the cameras and freeze the feed, so for all intents and purposes nothing untoward could be seen on the cameras. Had some observant person looked closely at the monitors they may have realized that not a frond of grass or a single leaf on a tree was moving in the slight breeze we had that day. Once Brian had frozen the feed he told the guy that the emergency was over and he didn't need to talk with Martinez after all."

"Crafty bastard," Martinez said, "he used my own resources against me."

"Not for the last time I'm afraid." De Sousa added.

"So, once the video feed was frozen we were able to drive up the road to the command post and wait for the delivery of the vans from the three pick-up points. We didn't want to risk leaving for the mansion before they arrived because the timing would have been off, so we kept everything as if it was going as per your schedule, just in case you had someone watching out for them. Once they turned up the men positioned themselves in the truck and prepared for the invasion of your home. The rest you know. Up until that point everything had proceeded like clockwork and we didn't know all the wheels were falling off until the truck, the money, Beasley and Brown all went missing." De Sousa finished speaking, stared at Martinez, and slowly shook his head. He was a beaten man and Martinez knew it.

"So when you say Gracie went missing, are you implying that she is a victim here?" Martinez asked looking a little perplexed.

"Not quite sure, Diego," De Sousa replied. "We searched their apartment as soon as Beasley's disappearance became apparent. The beds were made in both bedrooms and there was no evidence of a hasty getaway, her clothes were in the wardrobe of one bedroom and Beasley's were in the main bedroom."

"Ae you suggesting they slept in separate rooms?" Martinez asked looking even more confused.

"Their relationship was purely platonic, as her sole purpose was to act as a go-between for us and Beasley." De Sousa replied.

"Let me tell you something Manuel." Martinez said. He leant forward, rested his arms on the table, clasped his hands together and continued. "Yes, we did have surveillance on both of them. And yes we did have listening devices hidden in their apartment. On the day of the robbery our man saw Beasley drive the Honda from the underground car park but he never saw Gracie leave the apartment. But I can also tell you this, based on the sounds that were reported to me being heard coming from the bedroom I can assure you that their relationship was anything but platonic."

CHAPTER 23

A New Partnership

"So it appears they have both gone rogue," De Sousa said shaking his head. "That man Beasley has the charm of a Svengali. He could talk the hind legs off of a burro. They were supposed to appear to be a loving couple, not actually be an item. The poor girl probably fell under his spell while he was preparing for the heist."

"So are you saying that the girl has no culpability in these proceedings?" Martinez asked quizzically. "You're not saying she should be exempt from any punishment when we capture them?"

"Diego, I'm not sure of anything anymore." de Souza replied, then he perked up and looked directly at Martinez. "You said we. Are you suggesting we work together on this?"

"I believe that is what you are here for isn't it?" Martinez said but the question wasn't really being asked. "I will catch them Manuel, eventually, with or without the help of the police. But joining forces may provide us with a more expedient outcome."

"I wish I could help Diego but right now I'm a force of one. I'm more than happy to assist but I don't know what I could do." De Sousa said almost apologetically.

"Nonsense! Not only are you a good policemen but you still have contacts, friends in the force who know you are innocent of these accusations. They would still help you." Martinez understood the man was down, his self-esteem and his confidence were as low as they could get. "It is not unprecedented for the police to work with their adversaries to apprehend a criminal element that neither want on their patch. Scotland Yard worked with the London underworld to keep out the Mafia. Brazilian authorities have often worked closely with certain individuals to keep the balance of power. Hell, Manuel, don't you remember years ago when we worked together to keep out that Columbian gang?"

"Yes I do." De Sousa replied and smiled as he recalled that coup. "I got promoted for that little triumph."

"And you were totally honest about where your information came from weren't you?" Martinez demanded to know.

"Yes, I told them it was you. But they didn't care because we had nabbed the gang leaders." De Sousa said proudly.

"Exactly, and history can be repeated, Manual." Martinez was getting excited, a trait he very rarely exhibited. He leaned forward and banged on the desk to emphasize his point. "When I locate that little bastard, and locate him I will, he's yours. I will tell you where he is and you can go to your bosses and nab him. Your reputation will be restored, the suspension will be lifted and you can retire a happy man." Martinez sat back, smiling confidently at the policeman. De Sousa considered this for a while. Martinez was prepared to give him Beasley on a plate, for what purpose? So De Sousa asked, "I get Beasley but what do you get out of it Diego?"

There was a pause while Martinez pondered this then he coolly replied.

"I am out of pocket to the tune of over 1.5 million U.S. dollars. I want to be recompensed so that a portion of any money that is recovered needs to end up in my coffers. All the money stolen is in cash, so that should not be a problem." Martinez waited for a response from De Sousa.

"That may be difficult Diego but, as with this case, we do have a history of losing evidence and we certainly cannot necessarily be held responsible for the honesty of the police looking after any recovered cash," De Sousa replied. Martinez tilted his head slightly as if to say 'now you're talking'.

"One more thing," Martinez said.

"What's that?" De Sousa replied. Martinez leaned back, joined the tips of his fingers together as if he was praying and said, "I also want the girl."

CHAPTER 24

A Voice from the Past

"Diego," De Sousa said shaking his head, "I can't guarantee that. She's a policewoman."

"Was a policewoman." Martinez snarled. "Now she's a criminal, but she is not the big fish here. She is just a pawn, someone that Beasley used to achieve his objective. He will probably drop her like a lead balloon at his earliest convenience. No, Manuel, you get Beasley and some of the money. I get my expenses, plus a little interest and the girl."

De Sousa thought about this for a while. The facts were that when push-came-to-shove, if and when they did capture the duo, circumstances may well be out of both of their control.

"I will certainly do my best regarding the girl, Diego," De Sousa said reluctantly.

"Don't worry Manuel. She will not be harmed, and like a prison sentence, eventually she will be freed, with a little money in her bank account, to travel whereever her heart desires."

"I don't think that's an appropriate fate for someone who was just doing her job" De Sousa said trying to defend Gracie.

"But she didn't do her job did she?" Martinez sneered. "She crossed us both."

"Yes, but there were mitigating circumstances." De Sousa countered. "We underestimated Beasley's persuasive powers."

"Precisely. That is why we are giving her the benefit of the doubt. She doesn't go to prison and she leaves here with her record unblemished."

Martinez outstretched his arms as if to say "what is the problem?" He continued, "anyway, she will love it here. During her previous visits she was enthralled with the garden and wildlife. I'm sure that will give her an amusing pastime during her stay with us." De Sousa shuddered at the thought of what may be expected of the poor girl during her 'stay' but before he could dwell on it Martinez was all business again.

"So, Manuel, where are we with the police investigations? Your people can monitor all the border crossings and airports far better than I can. I'm assuming they have found nothing." Martinez said.

"Nothing." De Sousa confirmed. "I just can't get my head around how two people, a truck, a car and all that money can just disappear. We have carried out searches in every garage, building, and warehouse between the command post, and here at your mansion. We have reviewed all the video recordings we can get our hands on and seen fleeting glances of the truck coming and going on game day but since then, nothing. We checked the videos again thinking maybe they had somehow disguised the truck, but again, nothing we could pinpoint."

"It is unlikely they could have sprayed the vehicle." Martinez surmised. "Our surveillance teams would have noticed them bringing in the equipment somewhere and there was no evidence of that."

"Right," said De Sousa, "but could they have boarded up the side somehow?"

"Again, unlikely. There were no tools or materials to disguise the van." Martinez said. "What about the Honda? Did you get a sighting on that?"

"Same thing. We checked out all the videos we could find. One problem is the sheer number of vehicles on the road matching that make and model. We pursued what we could but we got nowhere. Now so much time has passed, the police are returning most of the manpower they have assigned to this case back to normal duties. It won't be long before this is a cold case, if you can believe that," De Sousa said with not a little resignation.

"Well I won't give up. That man Beasley and his moll are not going to make a fool out of me and get away with it," Martinez said angrily, his face contorting into a mask of anger that would put the fear into anyone. "He will be caught, Manuel, if it is the last thing I do. We are still in contact with all the forgers we know in Rio in case the pair are after new identities. There is not a man or women working the illegal border-crossings trade that won't report to me if they think these two are trying to get away."

"But what if they are already out of the country?" De Sousa asked almost pleadingly. "How in God's name will we find them?"

"There's still the question of the money. How could he get that much money out of the country?" Martinez asked.

"Maybe he hasn't. Perhaps he converted just an innocuous amount into various currencies with the view of returning on a regular basis to retrieve the rest when the dust has settled." Martinez mused.

"No. He had worked in a bank, albeit briefly, but to a criminal mind like his he probably learned all the angles during his short tenure. He probably set up various accounts, somehow deposited the money and transferred it somewhere. Probably to the same Swiss bank account where he stashed his original take." De Sousa said.

"But there were just the two of them. How would they get that much hard cash into the bank without some questions being asked?" Martinez asked. "Especially when the banks knew that a large amount of their money was out there somewhere begging to be deposited."

"I have no idea, Diego," De Sousa replied in frustration. "If I did we might have already caught the bastard by now."

They were both at their wits-end for now and their conversation stalled. De Sousa ran his fingers through his hair trying to think of something else they might have missed between them and Martinez just sat there drumming his fingers on his desk. De Sousa took a final swig of whiskey, emptying the glass just as Eduardo reappeared. De Sousa thought maybe he was returning to replenish his drink but instead he walked over to Martinez with a cell phone in his hand. Martinez looked at it and whispered, "it's Beasley."

CHAPTER 25

A Realization

Martinez put the phone on speaker and indicated to Eduardo that he wanted Deluca back in the room. "You're a dead man Beasley." Martinez said tersely in English as Deluca returned quietly and sat at Martinez's right arm. He nodded to De Sousa to acknowledge his complicity in the proceedings.

"Aw come now Diego, don't be so ungrateful." The three men in the room all looked at each other in complete surprise, Beasley had replied in flawless Portuguese. Up until then they were all under the impression Beasley possessed only a rudimentary knowledge of the local language. He could have picked up enough of the language to get by during his stint at the command post and dealing with the locals around his apartment but this was fluent. That changed everything.

"You haven't been charged with anything have you?" Beasley asked.

"Where's my money?" Martinez asked threateningly.

"Your money Diego? Don't you mean our money?" Brian replied with a laugh. If only he could have seen the blood rise in Martinez's face giving him a bright, red, evil appearance it might have altered his attitude. It certainly had changed the demeanors of Deluca and De Sousa, who were now sitting in the room fidgeting, no longer listening-in on a comfortable chat on the phone. They both knew what Martinez was capable of and the mood he was in right now did not bode well for anyone. But Martinez recognized that saying anything in his current state might result in revealing something he could regret so he just remained silent and let Beasley do all the talking.

"I decided that the original split was not to my liking and, of course, as you may have realized by now, I also took on an apprentice, so I decided I needed a bigger cut. I also figured that without my testimony they couldn't hang anything on you. So, Diego it has all worked out well for everyone except the banks and that old fart De Sousa. I understand he has recently been suspended." Beasley then laughed. This had the effect of placating Martinez and now making De Sousa the elephant in the room. Martinez thought that De Sousa was going to shout some obscenities down the phone, so Martinez rose from his chair, another act he rarely did in the middle of a meeting. He got into De Sousa's face and placed his forefinger to his own lips to indicate to him to remain quiet. Then he slowly sat back down holding both his hands palms outwards and towards De Sousa in a calming gesture.

"Where's my money?" Martinez repeated equally as menacingly as the last time.

"And I thought we were going to have a pleasant chat about old times and what I have been up to since we last met," Beasley said, still in a jocular manner. "Oh well, never mind. I'm sure Deluca is with you. If he's not, tell him to look in the 'pits'. He'll know where I mean. The money is there, what's left of it." Beasley then terminated the call. All eyes in the room turned to Deluca. He slowly turned to look at Martinez and merely nodded his head once.

CHAPTER 26

Some Redemption

"The 'pits'?" Martinez asked. "O.K. Deluca, Where the hell are the 'pits'?" Martinez had used Deluca's last name, never a good term of endearment, and not David.

"It is the building next door to the command post." Deluca replied uncomfortably.

"You've got to be kidding me." Martinez replied. "Are you trying to tell me they have been with the money, under our very noses the whole time?" Martinez said angrily.

"Why exactly do you call it the 'pits' David?" De Sousa said quietly trying to bring some calm back into the room.

"It used to be a workshop, so there are six pits in the ground so that cars can drive over them for oil changes, things like that," Deluca replied meekly.

"Oh my God, that's brilliant." De Sousa said. "So while we were scouring the city for a truck and a car they were holed up next door with all the money sitting right there in the ground. That's brilliant."

"Did you think to even look in the buildings along there?" Martinez demanded.

"We did and we found nothing. Like De Sousa said, we were looking for a car or a truck. We had no reason to enter every building and look for all that money stashed away. Who would have suspected they were holed up next door?" Deluca said defensively.

"No Diego, David is correct." De Sousa intervened. "My men also checked those buildings and we had no reason to suspect anything untoward," De Sousa added. "You know, now I think about it, a couple of weeks after the game we had a couple of tip-offs from locals in the town, fairly close to the command post regarding a man answering the description of Beasley."

"Did you pursue them?" Martinez asked brusquely.

"No. We asked if he spoke to them and they said 'yes', in very good Portuguese, so we thanked them and dismissed the calls," De Sousa told Martinez. "We were searching for someone who could only speak a little of the language but of course now it all makes sense. If only...." De Sousa's voice trailed off as he contemplated what might have been.

"Don't be too hard on yourself Manuel. We made exactly the same mistake," Martinez said, a little calmer now. But the statement brought a surprised look to De Sousa's face. Both Martinez and De Sousa were now beginning to realize just how good their foe really was, as they had both had the wool pulled over their eyes. For a moment they all sat there shaking their heads in disbelief. It was Martinez who made the first move. He placed both of his large hands on the table, rose and said, "take me to the 'pits'. Now." Not for the first time that evening Martinez was breaking tradition. This time he would be leaving the sanctuary of the mansion, something he rarely did. Maybe a funeral for a fallen operative, a family wedding or a court appearance but he did not make a habit of travelling beyond his own protective confines.

All three men travelled in the rear of the limo that was being driven by the usual gorilla of a driver. Not a word was spoken during the forty minute journey and when they arrived at their destination the driver quickly got out of the car to open Martinez's door. With equal speed and agility Deluca leapt from the car to open the doors of the 'pits'. With the aid of a flashlight he found the mains switch and turned on the overhead lights. The fluorescent lights flickered and shone down just as Martinez and De Sousa walked in. There were a few laundry trolleys scattered around the floor of the old workshop but other than that there was nothing to indicate anyone had been there. But all four men were more concerned with the location of the money and because Beasley had referred to the 'pit' they all assumed the money was in the ground. As a result, they centered their attention on the steel doors in the ground, for a few seconds they just stared at the rusty old portals as if opening them would release something foreboding. Then Martinez pointed to the first bay that had a '1' stenciled on the concrete floor in front of the doors. The driver bent down and effortlessly pulled open the heavy metal door. The pit was empty, except for a 100 REAL bill positioned perfectly in the middle of its floor. They all sidled the couple of metres to the bay marked '2' and Martinez nodded. The driver opened the doors of that bay to reveal two 100 REAL bills also perfectly positioned in the middle of the pit, not on top of each other but a couple of bill widths apart. By the time they opened bay '3' to see the three 100 REAL bills positioned in the same format Martinez could hardly contain his anger. Bay '4' was no better and Martinez involuntary shouted out at the top of his voice, "I want Beasley's head."

Without waiting for instruction the driver opened bay '5' but this time the pit was stuffed full of REALs of various denominations, but mainly hundreds. This was enough to calm the big man down and also brought relief to everyone else in the room. Bay '6' was a repeat of bay '5' and they tried to estimate exactly how much cash was in the two bays.

"Whatever it is, it is not enough." Martinez growled.

"More to the point, how much is missing?" De Sousa asked.

"Check upstairs," Martinez commanded. Both Deluca and the driver responded immediately and ran upstairs, two at a time, to investigate. This left Martinez and De Sousa alone on the ground floor. Whether that was the intent of Martinez or just coincidence, he took the opportunity to ask the all-important question.

"Well, Manuel, what do you see?" Martinez was still surveying the money and didn't look round at the deposed policeman. There was a moment of hesitation as the years of police training conflicted with his current predicament. Just at that moment Deluca shouted down from upstairs. "They were living here. There's food, sleeping bags and all sorts of garbage left behind." This prompted De Sousa to reply.

"I received an anonymous tip-off as to the whereabouts of the fugitive's hold-out but when I arrived to investigate all I found was a few thousand REAL scattered around the floor of the building and evidence that suggested they had been living here for some time. I still have no idea where the bulk of the money is." De Sousa sounded almost relieved, as though a whole weight had been lifted from his shoulders. The weight was replaced by the consoling arm of Martinez, another first, the big man putting his arm around another human being other than that of someone who was female.

"David, get someone over here to pack up this money. Our friend here needs to organize a police investigation. Leve a few thousand scattered around," Martinez ordered. Deluca was immediately on the phone to arrange the transfer while Martinez and De Sousa returned to the car. As they reached the car Martinez's cell phone began to ring. He answered the call with "Yes." He then listened for a few seconds and ended the call.

"It still doesn't explain the rest of the money. I don't understand how they could move all that cash without either of us hearing about it." De Sousa said mystified.

"Maybe they will tell us when we catch them, Martinez said and, as he turned to face De Sousa, he was smiling.

CHAPTER 27

Events Begin to Unfold

De Sousa wasn't quite sure what Martinez was up to when he said 'they will tell us when we catch them' but he was confident the big man would not hold anything back from him. So he waited for a call from Deluca to let him know when his men had cleared the money from the inspection pits in the building. As per De Sousa's request they were to leave a few thousand REALs strewn over the floor for effect. On receiving the call from Deluca, De Sousa then contacted his boss to let him know he had received a tip from an informant and he needed to get a team of police over to the 'pits' to investigate. He was immediately re-instated and within an hour he was directing his men to carry out an investigation of the premises. A search upstairs revealed the living quarters Brian and Gracie had been occupying and a forensic team was summoned to carry out tests. Judging by the state of the fruit and vegetable peelings; and other items found amongst the garbage, they felt it had been merely a week or so since the pair had departed. Amongst the paraphernalia the police discovered upstairs there was nothing that revealed the whereabouts of the truck, the car or the two fugitives. However, a couple of police uniforms were found that had been modified with the words 'DELTA SECURITY' with logos to match. De Sousa immediately ordered a door-to-door inquiry of all the banks in Rio to ask if any of them had been dealing with representatives from Delta Security.

One of the first people to respond was Fernando Cortez, manager of one of the biggest branches of the country's largest banks situated in downtown Rio. De Sousa went to interview the man who explained to him a meeting that had been conducted with a Mr. Flávio Anderson. He was quite happy to accommodate Mr. Anderson's request because he felt the work he was carrying out was a wonderful act of kindness for the poor people of Rio.

"Anderson said he worked for a consortium called 'Rio's Raptors', a group created to help the poor people of Rio. It was a name coined by one of the women in the consortium, he told me," Cortez explained but De Sousa was unimpressed and remained impassive.

"Mr. Cortez, exactly what did you do for Mr. Anderson," De Sousa asked. Mr. Cortez explained the discussion they had and concluded with how the cash was to be delivered.

"Mr. Anderson would call us the day before a delivery with the approximate time that a company called Delta Security would deliver a bag of cash to us. We would have a small team of people available using electronic cash counters to itemize the notes and deposit them into an account we had created for the client. It was anticipated that there would be a few deliveries, then we could discuss ways to invest the funds for the future betterment of the poor people of Rio," Cortez explained with a smile before continuing. "Because we could consider this a charitable cause we also offered an attractive interest rate. When I reported the client acquisition to head office they bumped the interest rate up another half point. It may sound a little pretentious, but it has been quite the feather in my cap." Cortez was beaming by the time he had finished his explanation.

"Mr. Cortez, would you please check the balance of the account as it stands to-day?" De Sousa calmly asked.

"Certainly." Cortez replied and turned his body in sync. with his office chair to type in some data on the keyboard of his personal computer. After a few seconds De Sousa heard Mr. Cortez whisper. "Well that's strange, the balance seems to be zero." Cortez continued to type in characters but it was obvious he was having serious difficulty finding any trace of the deposited money anywhere in the bank's records.

"Mr. Cortez," De Sousa said. But the man kept on typing and uttering unrecognizable expletives. "Mr. Cortez," De Sousa said a little more firmly. Still the man continued to type. This time De Sousa stood and pulled the man's arm away from the keyboard. "Mr. Cortez. You won't find the money. It's gone," De Sousa said soothingly. Cortez merely looked at him in a daze.

"But I don't understand," Cortez said almost silently.

"How much interest had you paid to date?" De Sousa quietly asked, still holding the man's arm. "It must have been a few thousand I think. I could find out exactly." Cortez replied.

"Which has also gone?" De Sousa asked although he already knew the answer.

"Which has also gone," Cortez replied.

"It gets worse Mr. Cortez," De Sousa said, "you have paid out interest on money that had originally been stolen from you – and it has been stolen again." With that De Sousa rose and started to leave the room, then he stopped, turned and he furrowed his brow as he thought of something.

"By the way, I think it may have been Anderson who came up with the name 'Rio's Raptors'," De Sousa said.

"What makes you say that?" Cortez asked quite taken aback.

"Well, my Latin is a bit rusty but I think you'll find raptor is Latin for robber," De Sousa said as he turned to leave the bank and a very distraught Cortez.

"That feather in his cap is looking not a little frayed around the edges, now," thought De Sousa as he left the bank.

CHAPTER 28

A Body of Evidence

So now De Sousa was back in his office mulling over what he knew. He knew where the money had been stashed between the day of the heist and when the money was being deposited into the various banks in Rio. He had designated people from the fraud squad to look into the trail of money from the time it left Beasley's bogus bank accounts, but that would take a few days before anything would emerge. De Sousa was still mystified as to how no traces of either the truck or the car had been found. During the interviews with the bank staff he had received a description of the van that had been used by Delta Security but it certainly didn't match that of the fruit and vegetable truck. No one had bothered to look at the license place so a trace could not be put on the vehicle. Needless to say a check on Delta Security came back negative, no reference to the company existed anywhere. So now the police were in the hunt for a third vehicle. Did they rent it? Buy it? Steal it? Where is it now? So many questions. Forensic had drawn a blank with their investigations at the 'pits'. It was obvious that Brian and Gracie had practiced the same habit of wearing latex gloves as there was not even a hint of a partial fingerprint in the place. It is possible they could extract DNA samples from the garbage left at the 'pits' and the sleeping bags to prove the perpetrators had been in the building but that wasn't much good without the capture of the bastards.

Beasley had obviously disguised himself as a Mr. Flávio Anderson and visited various banks to shift the cash from the 'pits' to the banks in a van claiming to be from Delta Security. From the descriptions received, the two occupants of the security van were more than likely Brian and Gracie, but all they could base that on was their height. Even then it was dubious while they were wearing helmets and riot boots. Obviously, Delta Security was a fictitious company but the van was real and where was it now? De Sousa tried to think the whole thing through from the day of the heist until the present. So now they knew that the money had been stashed right under their very noses. Brian and Gracie had holed up in the 'pits' until the dust had settled – but the disappearance of the truck, car and empty sports bags remained a mystery. Just at that moment one of his subordinates, a young policeman, entered his office.

"Penny for them boss," the man asked as he saw De Sousa staring into space.

"What's that?" Said De Sousa, returning from his personal reverie.

"Penny for your thoughts. You looked as though you were miles away there. Anything I can help you with?" The young policeman's name was Carlito Hernandes a hunk of a man at 6 feet 2 inches and muscular with it. After regular police training he had volunteered for the BOPE team and passed with flying colors. It didn't hurt that he was also a very bright young fellow with a degree in psychology.

"I was just going over the whereabouts of these two thieves. We have no trace of them right now." De Sousa said.

"That's a conundrum in itself sir but what gets me is how these bankers could be so gullible and not see through Beasley's cock and bull story. He's bringing them millions in cash how can they be that stupid?" Hernandes said.

"Ah, human nature I'm afraid." De Sousa replied. "Beasley spun a credible story and played on their compassion but of course the underlying pinion was their greed. The bankers saw this as an opportunity to climb the ladder of success and it blinded them to the fact that it was only a few weeks previous that millions of dollars had gone missing. They failed to put two and two together, bankers, go figure. The dollar signs in front of their eyes clouded their vision, again a great deal of that could be attributed to Beasley's persuasive power. He is after all a master manipulator."

"But to keep it so quiet, surely some of the bosses should have put two and two together, they hadn't even met Beasley." The policeman had put forward a good point.

"Yet again, credit must be given to Beasley." De Sousa replied with an appraising smile and a pointing finger. "The story about a bank fiddling the books and the need for absolute secrecy ensured that, apart from their bosses, the bankers kept their cards close to their chests. As a result, none of the other banks were aware that the consortium was dealing with all of them, each bank thought they had exclusive rights. On top of that, the bank managers merely told their bosses that they had won a new lucrative account. Not one of them told their bosses they were dealing with cash only transactions. They didn't need to and the fact that the consortium was dealing with street vendors was a convincing enough excuse for the cash. No, Beasley was clever, he knew they would fall for it." There was a pause in their conversation before De Sousa began to talk out loud.

"Pieces of the puzzle are beginning to fall into place but still I can't get past the disappearance of the truck and their car. Dammed if I can." De Sousa said.

"It's like an illusion isn't it sir?" Hernandes said honestly.

"Illusion, how do you mean?" De Sousa asked.

"Well sir, when I was a kid I remember once going to an elaborate magic show and there was this elephant on the stage. It was a real, live elephant and he was pissing on the floor, splashing everywhere it was. I was young and I thought it was hilarious, my mum was trying to keep me quiet but I couldn't help laughing." The man was relating the story like a joke and De Sousa was grinning with him, a welcome interlude to the pressure he had been under of late. The policeman was a young hardworking honest cop and he reminded De Sousa of himself when he was that age. He continued to humor him.

"So what happened?" De Sousa asked, relatively interested in the outcome by now.

"Well sir, the magician shouted out a command and suddenly the house lights went out, just for a second, the auditorium was pitch black and you couldn't see a thing." The young policeman was adding the theatrics now with hand movements, "and it was only a second, no more than that but when the lights came back on, the elephant and the piss were all gone; they had simply disappeared. But they couldn't have just disappeared could they sir? But where the hell did it all go? They must have still been there somewhere but the audience just couldn't see it." Hernandes stopped relating the story and stood there looking amazed as though it had just happened in front of his very eyes and not all those years ago.

"Of course they were still there," De Sousa said, still laughing at the story. "Were there bars around the stage for the audience's protection?" De Sousa asked.

"Yes, as a matter of fact there were, if I remember rightly, why do you ask?" Hernandes asked.

"Well, I was once investigating a case that required the services of a magician and he let me in on the secret of such a trick," De Sousa replied. "The bars weren't there for your protection they were the illusion. When the lights went out the bars flipped and when the lights came back on the gaps between the bars, through which you had been watching the elephant, were now closed. What you were now looking at was a picture of an empty stage painted on the slats that now filled the gaps between the bars. The elephant, as you so rightly said, was still standing in the same place but now it was concealed. Simple really, the difficulty would have been painting the slats to look exactly like the empty stage or making the stage look like the slats." De Sousa sat back quite proud of his explanation to his young novice who was now looking even more amazed. But the policeman still looked a little confused so De Sousa had an idea. He rose from his chair and walked to the window.

"Carlito, a little demonstration. Imagine these Venetian blinds are your bars on the stage. What do you see out of the window?" De Sousa asked.

"I see the windows of the building across the street." Hernandes replied. With a slick pull on the blind's lines De Sousa closed the blinds.

"What do you see now?" de souse asked.

"Nothing but the closed blinds." Hernandes said but he now looked more confused than ever.

"Exactly, nothing. Now, imagine if I had accurately and skillfully painted the same view on these blinds as you could see when they were open. A quick glance at them and you would believe the blinds were open because you could see the windows of the building across the street. Right?" De Sousa said as he opened the blinds once more and returned to his seat.

"Oh gotcha." The policeman said quite impressed. "Such a simple trick."

"All tricks are simple when you know how." De Sousa responded.

For a few seconds neither of them said anything. They just remained there smiling, then suddenly, De Sousa, who had been sitting back in his chair still enjoying the tale suddenly sat forward. His face lit up and he shouted, "that's it!"

"What's it?" Hernandes said somewhat surprised.

"You hit the nail on the head. It was all an illusion. We now know that the money was there all along, and so were they, ergo so was the truck and the Honda. We have been working under the assumption that they drove away somewhere and hid themselves with the truck and the money." De Sousa was beginning to get excited as a light went on in his head and he continued with his new theory. "But they didn't, they were right there the whole time. They gave us the illusion that they had driven off. After unloading all that money into the pits they would have had no time to drive the truck anywhere. It must still be somewhere in the vicinity. Well done young fellow, now get some men together. I want to do another search of the buildings and the surrounding area." De Sousa stood to retrieve his hat and headed enthusiastically for the car pool, hurriedly followed by six armed policemen.

It was a Sunday afternoon, so the traffic was comparatively light and with all sirens blaring it didn't take long for the cavalcade of police to reach the old command post. They searched the buildings again, but their findings were just the same as before, and De Sousa's enthusiasm began to dwindle once more. But then one of the policeman walked to the last building in the row where there was an old car park. The asphalt had not been maintained so it was cracked and pitted with the protrusion of weeds and young saplings. He studied it for a moment and then called out.

"Over here sir," the policeman shouted. He waited for the rest of the team to arrive and he pointed to some bushes near the edge of the river. The whole edge of the river was covered in foliage but some of it had obviously been disturbed. There were two gaps in the vegetation that could well have been made by a large heavy truck driving over it. The penny dropped.

"They drove the truck into the river," De Sousa said, standing there arms akimbo looking at the river as though it was obvious to everyone.

Immediately De Sousa was on the phone arranging for a team of divers to be dispatched to investigate the bottom of the river. Because of the lateness of the day it was agreed that they would have to start first thing in the morning, if the truck was there it wasn't going anywhere, another day was not going to make a difference. Bright and early the next morning an entourage of vehicles made its way to the disused car park, the occupants of the vehicles began to unload their equipment. Before long four police divers equipped with dry suits and heavy duty underwater lighting, to counteract the murky depths of the Guandu River, stepped off the river bank and into the water. There was a support team and additional divers to spell the other divers or to offer assistance. The diving team's leader, Captain Adriano Alves, remained on shore and explained to De Sousa that it could be difficult to locate the truck, even if it was there at all, because of the current, depth and poor visibility. But they would give it three days and if they couldn't locate it, well he was afraid they would have to call off the search. He had only agreed to doing this now because he and De Sousa went way back a long way and he trusted the experienced policeman's hunches. De Sousa liked Adriano and he knew he was one of the most experienced divers in the world. He wasn't a particularly tall man but he was thickset with a ruggedly handsome face. Early in his career he had received an invitation from the late Jacques Cousteau to participate in a diving expedition onboard the Calypso to visit Brazil's National Park, Fernando de Noronha, which of course he accepted. That certainly didn't hurt being part of his resume. Then later in his career he had participated in the United Nations' International Conference on Environment and Development in Rio de Janeiro working again alongside Mr. Cousteau.

Mid-afternoon of the first day one of the divers came up to the surface and called Alves over to the riverbank. They had a brief conversation before the diver submerged again under the murky depths; meanwhile, Alves organized a couple of his men to get a rope to follow the diver's instructions whenever he returned to the surface. De Sousa was watching the scene from the car park and Alves saw him looking at them so he turned and began to walk towards an eagerly expectant De Sousa.

"We found something Manuel, but you're not going to like it," Alves said.

"Why what is it?" De Sousa asked.

"It's a body and beside it, stuck in the mud, is a pistol," Adriano Alves replied. "You may have to add murder to the list of offences this guy has done."

CHAPTER 29

Missing Evidence Found

"Impossible," De Sousa said, "Beasley may be a crook but I can't see him resorting to murder; he doesn't have the stomach for it."

"Desperate men do desperate things Manuel," Alves replied, but by then De Sousa had turned to one of his men and said, "get on to homicide, tell them we have found a body in the river and to arrange for a team to get over here immediately." As the policeman turned to walk away and radio in the request De Sousa switched his attention back to Alves.

"I appreciate what you're saying Adriano but I don't think this has anything to do with Beasley. I don't think he was ever put in a position of desperation. Based on the evidence to date I think things went exactly as planned for him," De Sousa told Alves. Then they all turned their attention to the activities going on by the side of the river. On the riverbed the diver had tied the offered line around the body, underneath the body's lifeless armpits. The diver gave a tug on the rope which was the signal for the men on the riverbank to begin hauling the dead weight to the surface, assisted by some inflatable devices strategically placed around the body by the diver. Between them they manhandled the body onto dry land and the diver placed the pistol, equipped with a silencer, beside the dead man. The diver explained that normally the current would have taken the body downstream but it must have just fallen onto some old mangrove roots just beneath the surface of the river and got caught. As for the gun, it must have been loosely tossed into the river and the silencer went stem first into the mud and formed the perfect anchor. De Sousa walked towards the still form lying on the bank, which was highly decomposed and unrecognizable. Forensics would only be able to identify the body through DNA analysis or dental records. De Sousa would have to wait for homicide before knowing who the victim was and determine whether it was even related to his case. The only concern he had right now was the delay to the search for the truck and the effect this sideshow had on his timeline.

Fortunately, his fears were unwarranted, on the second day the truck containing the car and bags were located. Recovery, however, was a whole different ball game. The recovery team would have to get heavy-duty salvage machinery in place to extricate the truck from the depths of the filthy river and because of the remote location that in itself was going to be a challenge. By the time everything was in position it would be almost a month before the truck et al was finally salvaged from the river.

With the truck found there was no more De Sousa could accomplish at the diving site so he returned to continuing with the investigation from his office. A couple of days later the forensic team investigating the body that had been found in the river had identified the man and cause of death. The man's name was Pedro Garcia, a low-life bookie who had been involved in many run-ins with the law. Forensics had concluded he had been killed by a single gunshot to the head at close range. They also confirmed the gun that was found in the river was indeed the murder weapon, but the owner of the weapon was unknown, and it was unlikely they could track down any history as the gun's serial number had been filed off. A police report showed Garcia had been reported missing some time before the games began and the rate of decomposition on the body supported that time lapse, give or take a few days. After seriously considering this evidence De Sousa believed the body to be a red herring and deemed it had nothing to do with Beasley or the grand theft but he wanted to be sure. He left the office and walked a few blocks until he came to a convenience store he knew of that still maintained a pay phone, something which is difficult to find in this day and age. De Sousa was dressed in civilian clothes and the phone booth was partially concealed by billboards and parked trucks. He made calls from this phone regularly when he wanted to contact some of his informants or in this case Martinez because he could do it inconspicuously from an untapped phone. He dialed the number.

"Martinez." Came the reply.

"It's Manuel," De Sousa answered. "Diego, you're probably aware by now that we have found the truck and the car. They were dumped in the river at the back of the command post. But during the search one of the divers also found a body. The body has been identified as one Pedro Garcia, he'd been shot." Manuel stopped talking but there was predictably no reply from Martinez, so he continued. "The estimated time of death, although it is difficult to judge with some accuracy, puts it way before the day of the game. So I don't believe Beasley had anything to do with the murder." De Sousa stopped again but this time Martinez did reply.

"Garcia was the scum of the earth, the world is a better place with him not in it." Martinez said through clenched teeth almost spitting down the telephone line. "Beasley had nothing to do with his murder." Martinez didn't elaborate on who may have been responsible for the man's death and De Sousa didn't ask but Garcia must have done something seriously wrong to cause Martinez to talk like that. With nothing further to be said they merely both ended the call simultaneously.

So, thankfully, De Sousa dismissed the murder as part of his investigation and on his return to the office he let homicide know that it would be their responsibility to pursue the murderer or murderers. 'Good luck with that one', he thought; although, he had a pretty shrewd idea who was responsible for the death.

So now that they had found the truck it was all beginning to fit and the only question left to be answered was the whereabouts of Brian and Gracie? De Sousa was pretty much beating himself up on this point when a couple of breaks happened in the case that had the propensity to crack it wide open.

CHAPTER 30

New Evidence

De Sousa received a call from one of his men regarding the sighting of a suspicious looking vehicle parked in the long-term car park at the airport: a black van. They had received a tip-off in response to a bulletin released by the police that provided a description of the van based on their bank witnesses' testimonies. A diligent car park security guard had been listening in on the police wave band and discovered the van. He felt that a black windowless van amongst all the posh cars and high-end SUVs in the long term car park was a little unusual, so he notified a friend of his in the force.

A patrol car containing two policemen was dispatched to investigate and they used one of their myriad of tools to open the doors of the van. Inside, there were two bicycles but not much else to go on. However, while one of the policeman went into the van for a more thorough search his partner was radioing in the license plate and VIN. While he was doing that he saw evidence of a spray paint makeover on the side. He moved around to try and get different perspectives with what little light was being provided in the multi-story car park, but he could definitely tell the van had recently been spray-painted on the sides. Now, why, he thought, would both sides need to be painted and not the back or front of the vehicle? Unless something needed to be covered up. This provided enough evidence to confiscate the van so they arranged for a tow truck to come and take it to a local police station for further forensic investigation. Within a few hours, reports were being sent to

De Sousa that indicated it was the van used by Delta Security. The logo and name had been painted on in white and then later covered up with black spray paint. Other than that, there were no fingerprints and nothing was found that could indict Brian or Gracie on either the van or the bikes. A trace of the license plate had been fast-tracked and the last known owner was hunted down: it was the used car dealer in the local town next to the 'pits'. Detectives were sent to interview the salesman and they determined, although there was not enough evidence to stand up in court, it had been Beasley who had bought the van. The height and build were right but the hair and eye colors didn't match Beasley or Brown's profiles, although the timing of the purchase was in keeping with that of the bank deliveries. Which brought De Sousa round to contemplating the deliveries. The money arrived at the bank in laundry trolleys, most of which had been left at the banks. Where did the laundry trolleys come from? He assigned a couple of policemen to look in the local phone books to find stores that sold those particular trolleys. It didn't take long to isolate the only store in the area that supplied that type of laundry basket. Interviews with the store owner confirmed it was the same man who had purchased the van from the used car lot. The store owner went on to explain that he had helped the man load the trollies into a black van. But it still didn't do much good in contributing to the whereabouts of the fugitives. Except that now, because of the security cameras at the airport, they had a pretty good idea of when Brian and Gracie had arrived there. But to investigate which flight a man and a woman of their description had taken, as vague as they could supply, would take forever. That's when the second break came.

De Sousa's cell phone rang, it was Diego Martinez.

"De Sousa here," De Sousa said, surprised that Martinez would be phoning him during the day.

"I know where they are," Martinez replied and then immediately terminated the call.

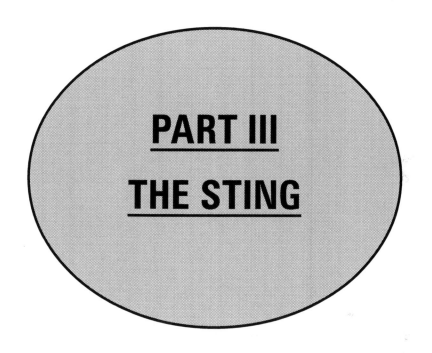

PART III

THE STING

CHAPTER 31

First Deception

It had all begun that day of the game. As far as everyone was concerned, everything was going to plan; that is until the truck arrived and Brian dismissed the rest of the command-post team. He was a little concerned when José dallied, which only confirmed his suspicions that he was a mole, but fortunately in the end he was persuaded to leave. With the video cameras disabled, Brian went outside to his car. It was a beautiful day and, as usual, he had left the sun roof open. Brian was whistling as he approached the SUV, which was a signal for Gracie to extricate herself from beneath the camping equipment in the Honda where she had been hiding. Brian opened the car door and Gracie slowly climbed out before performing a good stretch after being stuck in an undignified position for the last few hours. They hugged each other briefly.

"You O.K.?" Brian asked her affectionately as he passed her a sports drink and a pastry that Osvaldo had baked fresh only that morning.

"Fine, bit stiff but I'll loosen up once I start moving." Gracie replied, then her eyes lit up as she saw the food Brian was offering. "Oooh, is that for me?" It was a rhetorical question as she grabbed the pastry out of his hand and stuffed the whole thing in her mouth while attempting to smile at the same time.

"There are plenty others if you want some more," Brian said as he laughed at her antics. But then he stopped laughing as Gracie finished what was in her mouth and looked very seriously at him.

"Are you sure this is a good idea Brian? We can still back out you know, stick with the original plan and return home," Gracie questioned.

"What? And constantly be looking over our shoulders in case one of Martinez's men come after us," Brian replied.

"Martinez is going to be coming after you now no matter what you do Brian. Only, if you stick to the plan he will be in jail and his power diminished significantly." Gracie pleaded.

"There would still be Deluca. Together with the muscle of his big buddy he would pick up the reins and the whole organization would not skip a beat," Brian explained, "but this way, Martinez stays out of prison, he gets a whole slew of cash and we will be filthy rich."

"But all the risks that are involved Brian." Gracie appealed.

"Look, I've been over this a thousand times. It's going to work like Swiss clockwork. Look at me," Brian demanded as he stood back to let her look at him. "Do you see any nerves or concerns?" Brian asked. Gracie just shook her head and smiled.

"No, of course not. We are going to do this. Now are you sure you wouldn't like another doughnut before those policemen arrive and finish them off?" Brian asked her. He saw her laugh as she melted under his charms.

"Later, let's get on with what we have to do before they get here," Gracie replied. Then she unscrewed the bottle top of the cold drink Brian had brought for her and took a long swig. Gracie screwed the top back on and tossed the bottle through the sun roof into a bag in the rear of the car. She then proceeded to carry some of the contents of the car into the building adjoining the command post, the one referred to as the 'pits'. First, she wheeled Brian's bicycle to the door of the building that Brian had just unlocked and opened. While Brian returned to the command post Gracie carried the bicycle up the gantry stairs and parked it in one of the rooms. She then returned to the car for her bicycle before making another trip for the sleeping bags, mattresses and cooking gear that were stored in the back of the Honda.

On those evenings and week-ends that Brian had worked alone, he had used the opportunity to scout out his surroundings. Using the rear fire exit from the gantry in the command post, undetected by the security cameras, he left the command post and broke into the adjoining building. He discovered that this building had a similar set-up. It had active power outlets, hot and cold running water, a washroom and a shower. Not quite as sophisticated as the command post, but still functional. In addition, the gantry upstairs was not open-plan: it had walls that had been used for storing spare parts and tools. It was because this building had been designed for a motor repair shop and these rooms were used as store rooms for the spare parts. The ground floor was completely open, except it had six bays for servicing cars. The bays had originally been set up for power ramps so that vehicles could be raised to any level for servicing or repairs. The ramps had long gone but the servicing pits remained, covered by steel plate doors and struts to prevent someone accidently falling into them. Each pit was three metres long, 1.5 metres wide and 1.5 metres deep. This of course started to get Brian's conspiritorial juices flowing and he began to form a counter-plan.

Gracie was laying out the sleeping equipment in one of the upstairs room of the adjoining building while Brian began to extricate all the cash from the ATMs in the command post. Once Gracie had transferred the things they needed from the car to the upstairs rooms she went to the command post. By now Brian had taken out all the cash from the ATMs and stuffed it into a large canvas bag. Gracie took the bag and returned to the building next door to empty the contents of the canvas bag into the corner of one of the rooms upstairs. She needed to empty the bag for a return trip for the rest of the money; the contents of the ATMs required a couple of trips to stash all the money in the adjoining building. Next, Gracie retrieved a large cooler from the Honda and in the command post they began to empty the contents of the refrigerator into the cooler. Gracie took the full cooler next door to empty as Brian brought up the rear carrying the microwave. Gracie emptied the contents of the cooler into the sink and returned to gather more supplies from the refrigerator. This time Brian followed her back, carrying the electric kettle and toaster. They were working together like a well-conducted orchestra: they had rehearsed this so many times on their camping trips and had developed a count for each trip. On the second trip Gracie had to place the food from the cooler into the shower stall as the sink was now full. On the third trip Brian brought back cooking utensils, the coffee maker and a few dry supplies. Once the refrigerator was empty they wheeled the appliance to the edge of the stairs. This was going to be the tricky part. Brian went to the Honda for a long strong rope that they had used during one of their camping trips. He tied one end of the rope to a load-bearing girder at the top of the stairs. Between them they then put the refrigerator on its side and Brian hooked the rope around its base. Brian then looped the rope around the top metal staircase strut supporting the bannister; this would take most of the load as they slid the appliance down the stairs. Brian glanced briefly at Gracie; she was ready so he nodded his head. That was the cue for them to both gently push the refrigerator down the stairs. Simultaneously Brian provided some slack on the rope as the refrigerator used its own weight to gravitate to the ground. Just as the back castor wheels of the refrigerator touched ground Brian secured the rope. Brian and Gracie, who were both sweating profusely by now, walked down the stairs, then heaved the appliance back to its upright position. Now, in its normal position, it was easy to quickly wheel it to the adjoining building. The good news was that the building next door was equipped with a chain and tackle that was used to remove motor engines from any one of the six bays. So once the refrigerator was secured with the chains lifting it to the top floor it only took a couple of minutes. At the top of the stairs they undid the lifting tackle and wheeled the refrigerator into one of the rooms and positioned it against the wall close to an electrical outlet. Gracie plugged it back in and power was restored. They had to make two more trips together to retrieve a laser printer, some packets of print paper, a couple of spare ink cartridges and some miscellaneous kitchen items. Once the equipment was safely stored away they stood and recited their memorized check-lists to verify that they had fulfilled all their objectives for this phase of the plan. Satisfied, Brian and Gracie quickly hugged, kissed, then wished each other luck. Brian went back down the stairs, locked the door on his way out and returned to the command post. Meanwhile, Gracie began replenishing the refrigerator and positioning the appliances Brian had retrieved. She arranged the appliances and other items they had brought up and once she was satisfied that their new home, albeit temporary, was ship shape she finished her drink that had been tossed into the bag of clothes in the car, then she lay down to try and relax, at least for a few hours.

Gracie found relaxation was difficult to come by. She was lying on her sleeping bag with her hands behind her head staring up at the grimy ceiling wondering how she had gotten herself in this deep. She was participating in a crime that, if caught, would probably mean she would never return home again. How could she have been so easily persuaded to even consider what she was doing, let alone aiding and abetting the felon she was supposed to be monitoring? She knew the answer to that: she fell in love with him. When exactly it was when she realized she was in love with Brian she couldn't really pinpoint, but it could have easily have been as early as the interviews in the prison. They made love that first night they slept in their apartment on their arrival in Rio and from there their affair just blossomed: at least that's how Gracie felt about it. Gracie believed Brian had sensed that and, as he began to concoct his plan, he didn't think for a minute she wouldn't do anything he asked. But this was the point of no return for her. She could make an appearance when the first of the task force arrived and no one would be aware of the potential subterfuge. Brian and she could leave together, her police record would be intact and she could return home. If anything, her participation as an undercover policewoman in a global operation would garner her awards and promotion. Brian and she could still live happily ever after, if, that is, Brian felt the same way she did, and despite what Brian had said to the contrary regarding Martinez's organization. She was still weighing up the alternatives when she heard a car arrive.

The arrival of Deluca was completely unexpected and with the imminent arrival of the police, Brian had to think of a way to get rid of him. Brian's heart was racing a mile a minute when Deluca began to question the whereabouts of José; it further strengthened what Brian had suspected all along. There was a mole in the team and it was José. By spreading the germ of an idea that José didn't really want to be there was a good enough reason for Deluca to leave in a huff to pay the man a visit.

When Deluca left, Gracie's thoughts were again racing. She knew he wasn't supposed to have been there and they had gotten away with one.

Here they were at the starting post, and they were almost busted. She was still betwixt and between revealing herself to call off Brian's sting when she heard the approach of some more vehicles, but this time it was De Sousa and his men.

It was 3:15 PM when De Sousa arrived with a squad of his men. De Sousa came to talk with Brian, although his men didn't even acknowledge him as they went directly to the fruit and vegetable truck to reconnoiter. There were ten of them there already and they would be joined by six more when the cars containing the money from the pick-up points arrived.

"Everything going as planned Brian?" De Sousa asked cordially.

"Better than expected in fact," Brian replied. He was back in the climate-controlled command post and he had cooled down from the exertions of moving stuff to the next door building and the anxiety from Deluca's unexpected visit. "Take a look at these stats." Brian indicated the numbers on the monitors as the amounts kept climbing in front of their eyes. "If anything, I think we are ahead of schedule." Brian added.

"Wonderful, I think we have him this time." De Sousa said.

"One thing you might like to be aware of." Brian said as he monitored the figures on the screens.

"Oh yes, what's that?" De Sousa asked with concern.

"Deluca was here earlier, he said he was going to check in on the pick-up centers." Brian replied.

"No problem, we anticipated that and we have a lookout for him at each of the centers. If he shows up and enters any of the centers he will be arrested. An added bonus." De Sousa replied enthusiastically.

"Sir, one more thing." Brian said as De Sousa turned to look at him, "I have been thinking, I would like to be there when you capture Martinez. I would like to see the look on his face as he is finally taken down."

"Not a good idea Brian." De Sousa replied shaking his head. "It could be dangerous, the heavies Martinez employ are not afraid to use their weapons, even against the police. Bullets could be flying everywhere. I would hate to see you injured, or worse, after all the good work you have done."

"I could wear a protective suit and a helmet just like your guys and I could keep down low in the cab until it is all over. Anyway you might need me to drive the truck, remember, the operative assigned to drive the truck is known to the guards on the gate." Brian explained, "they won't recognize your guy but they would recognize me." De Sousa mulled that over for a few seconds and then said.

"You make a good point Brian, but have you had any experience driving a big rig like that?" De Sousa asked.

"Worked on farms back home, I can handle that." Brian replied but De Sousa was skeptical. Nevertheless De Sousa left the command post to ask some of his men if they had spare suits in their cars. A couple of minutes later De Sousa returned with some suits.

"Here, try on one of these BOPE suits. I have brought various sizes for you to try. I know you will be in the cab but bullets have been known to stray. Make sure that once you are through the gates of the mansion put your helmet on. Is that understood?" Brian nodded his agreement and De Sousa patted him on the shoulder.

Brian took the suits upstairs to the washroom to select one that was an appropriate size. He decided on the medium size one: it was still a little too big, but it was functional. He selected the mid-size with the helmets that had been provided and returned downstairs leaving the other suits in the washroom. Now it was just a matter of waiting.

They watched the monitors as more and more ATMs were being drained of their contents. During this phase they were making idle chat but Brian was intrigued about one thing, so he asked De Sousa, "sir, with 700 operatives in the field was there anyone who informed the police of what was going down?"

"Ah. You don't know the power that Martinez has and the respect that the fraternity he lauds over has for him." De Sousa replied with almost respect. "There has not been a single report of anything going down to-day. Anyway, even if there was, we already knew about it, didn't we? No, this has been a closely guarded operation and it looks like being a complete success."

At 6:30 PM the last of the vans used for the pick-ups arrived at the command post amid cheers of derision from the squaddies. The van was driven through the open doors of the command post to join the other two vans already parked there. As the policemen were positioning themselves in the back of the fruit and vegetables truck Brian locked the doors of the command post. He then climbed into the driver's side of the cab just as one of the policemen jumped into the passenger side. Brian gave a toot on his horn which was responded to with a couple of bangs on the truck coming from the inside. This was to indicate they were all prepared and ready to leave. Brian put the rig into gear and with some trepidation began the drive to the mansion.

The drive to the mansion wasn't as bad as Brian thought it would be, driving large trucks was not exactly his forte, despite what he had told De Sousa. What Brian had told De Sousa was indeed true, he did have experience driving trucks on a farm during one of his school holiday working programs, although it was a few years ago now. But driving a big rig through traffic with all the wide turns he needed to perform was quite a different experience. Fortunately his passenger didn't suspect anything untoward and Brian continued as though he had been driving heavy goods vehicles all his life. Nothing was said between the two men in the cab on the way to the mansion, Brian was too busy concentrating on driving the rig and the policeman was too intent on listening to his hand-held police radio. That was another thing Brian had hoodwinked De Sousa into thinking, that the guards would recognize him. De Sousa should have realized Brian had actually only been to the mansion on a couple of previous occasions. Once in the back of Deluca's limo, where the guards couldn't have possibly seen him in the back with Gracie. The other occasion was for the garden party when he and Gracie had arrived in the Honda. The chances that the same guard would be on duty as he drove the rig through the gates were almost nil. Furthermore, it was unlikely that the operative who had been designated to drive the truck had ever been to the mansion. The bottom line was the guards were really only on the lookout for the fruit and vegetable truck, they were not interested in who was driving it. Brian was surprised De Sousa had been fooled that easily, he thought it would be at least a ten minute argument before he could oppose all the policeman's objections before finally convincing him.

As they neared the mansion the policeman was listening on the radio for the signal to proceed into the mansion which would be given once all three helicopters had safely landed at the helipad. Until then Brian had to proceed slowly and if necessary completely stop out of sight of the guards at the mansion. Once the go ahead was given the policeman was to conceal himself on the floor of the cab until they were through the mansion's gates. As soon as the call was given to leave the truck the policeman would jump from the cab and it would be Brian's turn to hide himself at the bottom of the cab until any shooting had stopped.

The departure of the truck from the command post was also Gracie's cue to leave the sanctuary of the upstairs rooms and commence the next phase of her tasks. If only Brian had known how close she had come to making an appearance earlier when De Sousa had arrived, which would have blown his scheme apart, but she hadn't.

It was dark now, so Gracie gingerly went down the stairs and took a peep out of the window. The truck had left, but just to make sure, she slowly opened the Judas gate in the door and peered outside. The area was deserted and in the dark she felt a little uncomfortable being in the middle of nowhere by herself. She turned on her powerful flashlight and got to work. Gracie opened the doors of both the command post and the building known as the 'pits'. She drove the first of the vans that were parked next door and reversed it to the first of the six pits. With great effort she opened the steel doors to the first pit and from the back of the van she began to empty the contents of all the money bags into the pit. She had now crossed the line and become a felon. Once all the bags had been emptied she then drove the van to just beyond the command post and drove the second of the vans to the pit and repeated the task of unloading. Towards the end of depleting the second van of its bags she realized the first pit was getting full. She closed the steel doors of the first pit, opened the steel doors of the second pit and began to fill it with the rest of the money from both the second and third van. She closed the doors of the second pit then drove the vans back into the command post in the order they were driven in. She locked the doors of the command post then, drove the Honda to the 'pits' and began to load all the empty money bags into it. She then returned the Honda to its parking spot and casually walked back to the building to relax for a little while.

At the same time Gracie was resting, Brian was waiting for De Sousa to enter the doors of the mansion with Martinez. Once De Sousa and

Martinez were inside the mansion he drove the truck across the grass over to the helipad. There were a number of people milling around over there, consisting of both policemen and a collection of Martinez's men under armed guard. Brian circled the truck until the rear of the trailer was adjacent to a pile of the money bags that had been taken out of the helicopter from Brasilia. The truck's tires left a few ruts in the finely manicured lawns but Brian thought that would be the least of Martinez's current problems. Brian halted the truck, climbed down from the cab and with great authority and perfect Portuguese Brian shouted, "De Sousa's orders. This money has to be transported immediately. Get it into the truck." Without questioning him, a couple of the policemen indicated with a swing of their guns that the captives, Martinez's men, should load the bags into the back of the truck. Brian started to load the bags and the others reluctantly followed suit until all the bags from all three helicopters had been loaded. Brian then thanked them, climbed back into the cab and drove towards the gates of the mansion.

CHAPTER 32

Removal of the Evidence

On the drive back to the command post Brian stopped at an overpass that crossed over a railway line. Underneath the bridge was a goods-train hauling a number of an open rail cars carrying coal. Brian had found the tracking bug on his Honda, which he was certain would be there, removed it and now tossed it on to the coal in the rail car. Brian then continued driving to the command post and as soon as Gracie heard his approach she opened the third of the pit bays in preparation for the truck load to be emptied. The unloading of the fruit and vegetable truck was going to take considerably longer to empty than the others, even though there would be two of them emptying the bags.

When Brian initially thought of the sting he had his doubts that the six pits could hold such a high volume of bank notes. But he took the measurements of the pits, calculated the volume required for the notes and was satisfied there would be enough room, albeit a tight fit. At worst, he would have to leave some money in the truck but after many iterations of calculations on his computer, re-checking and re-verifying his figures, he was certain the pits would hold the money. Obviously, there would be insufficient room for the bags as well, that would mean emptying the bags and disposing of them. That brought with it two more problems. The lack of time and the disposal of the bags. The disposal of the bags was simple, but emptying all those bags from the vans and the truck would be impossible by himself, that's why he decided to bring Gracie in on the plot. Needless to say, when he first approached her she considered the idea preposterous and would not entertain the notion, in fact in the beginning she thought Brian was joking. But he worked on her, by now he realized she was besotted with him and eventually her non-commitment turned into reluctance until finally she became a willing partner in the crime. During all his other crimes Brian had never worked with a partner before but assistance was essential during this plot and his plan was to discard the lady at a convenient juncture in the future.

Time was of the essence during this phase of the plan, Brian needed Gracie's help to make this happen. They had no knowledge of how long it would be before De Sousa or any of his men showed up. They had calculated approximately how long this exercise would take but the effort required to work quickly was very taxing. They worked without saying a word to conserve energy, because they knew if they stopped they were doomed. But so far, despite their weariness, they were slightly ahead of schedule. To speedily expedite the transfer of the bags Brian stood in the back of the truck tossing out the bags while Gracie emptied their contents into the pits. Once all the bags were out of the truck Brian helped Gracie empty the bags. Finally, the last of the bags was emptied and they turned their attention to stuffing the empty bags into the remaining spaces in both the Honda and the truck's spacious cab. Once that was almost finished, Brian left Gracie to continue with the stuffing of the empty bags into the cab while he went to the rear of the truck. The truck was equipped with pull-out ramps which the truck owner used for driving a forklift into the cargo hold when large palettes of goods were ordered. Brian needed the metal ramps for a completely different reason. He unlocked the safety catches holding the ramps in their channels and one by one pulled the two ramps out from their tracks and secured their leading edges on the ground. Brian then drove the Honda up the ramps and into the truck. Before he got out of the car he opened the windows and sun roof slightly then secured the emergency hand brake. He turned off the engine, put the gear shift in park mode and got out of the car leaving the keys in the ignition. Brian then jumped down from the truck and slid the ramps back into their concealed tracks. He closed one of the truck's rear doors and secured the other to the side of the truck using the built-in fasteners. He then returned to the front of the truck to help Gracie finish loading the empty money bags into the cab.

Once all the bags were stored in the truck, Gracie closed the doors of the building and proceeded to close the steel doors of all the bays while Brian drove the truck to the end of the long line of deserted buildings. At the end of the buildings amongst the overgrown wild vegetation was a patch of weed-strewn asphalt that was once used as a car park. He turned onto the patch and drove around in a circle until the back of the truck faced the edge of the river then he stopped. The truck was now parked at a slight angle, almost parallel to the river's current. Brian then reversed the truck until the wheels of the trailer were actually in the water. Here Brian stopped, he put the truck into park and took one of their tent's telescopic poles that had been stored in the back of the Honda and wedged it between the accelerator and the steering column. The truck's engine was now shaking on its mounts as it hit full revolutions. Brian opened the cab door, looked around to make sure his BOPE suit was not going to snare on anything. Brian was aware that this was the tricky part. Originally, his plan was to just drive the truck into the river but he realized that once the cab hit the water all forward propulsion would have been lost and the weight of the trailer rooted on land may have prevented the rig from going any further. Needless to say he felt it was necessary to reverse the truck into the water. Brian felt the car park here was large enough to drive in a complete circle and it would give him one shot to reverse it all into the river.

He put his foot firmly on the brake and moved the gearshift gingerly into reverse. He took a deep breath and leaped from the truck. Brian rolled on to the ground away from the truck, that had now lurched backward and the trailer part of the truck was no longer on dry land. He watched for a few seconds as the cab followed the trailer into the water. There was a loud roar as the drive wheels were spinning in mid-air and another one as the cool water hit the hot engine in a hissing spray of steam. Then the engine cut-out as water engulfed the fuel system. For a few more seconds the vehicle bobbed around in the current. Immediately the water began to pour through the truck's open doors and windows, filling every crevice and opening. Within a few more seconds the truck, Honda and money bags were completely immersed in the swirling murky Guandu River and out of sight.

CHAPTER 33

Laying Low

Brian and Gracie had now carried out the next phase of their plan to its fruition and all they could do now was wait patiently before they could finalize their remaining tasks, but that wouldn't be for a few days. Brian had set up another video camera, which he had found in a box in the command post. He positioned this one to monitor the road to the buildings. There was also a motion-detector which he set up close to the main road which that would activate an alarm on his laptop in the event that some unwanted intruders approached the buildings. The alarm would give Brian and Gracie adequate time to enter into their shut-down mode. When De Sousa and his men drove down the road in three separate vehicles with sirens blaring and lights flashing, he was pleased that both the camera and the motion detector alarm functioned perfectly.

Brian and Gracie's shut-down mode included verifying that everything was switched off in their building and that their laptops were closed. There was masking tape on the refrigerator's operating lights so that there was nothing to indicate to the outside world that anyone was in the building. The refrigerator was of the modern type and was almost silent while it was running. They didn't feel it was necessary to turn it off during a shut down mode. Brian certainly couldn't hear it from the command post when he was in the 'pits' during his trial runs prior to game day.

While De Sousa and his men checked out the command post Brian and Gracie lay quietly on the mattresses. They giggled together conspiratorially, albeit quietly, as they listened to the string of obscenities being shouted as the police realized all the money from the three vans had disappeared. They heard rather than saw someone checking the doors of the 'pits' as the doors were tested to see if they were locked and then they could see, seeping through a crack in the wall of the room they were in, the light of a flashlight being shone around the room. They could hear voices doing the same inspection with all the other buildings along the line. It was at this point that De Sousa must have realized that the truck and the Honda were definitely not there, so he quickly ordered the men back on the road and they swiftly retraced their steps in search of their quarry.

After The departure of De Souza and his men Brian and Gracie laughed, high-fived each other and drank a celebratory glass of champagne that they had stowed in the Honda. The bubbly had been purchased and stored in their apartment before finally transferring it to the refrigerator. They were hoping to find an appropriate moment to consume the beverage and they both agreed that this was it. They were halfway through their tipple when the detector alarm on Brian's laptop beeped yet again. Brian lifted up the screen to look at the image being sent from the video camera. It was Deluca's limo driving slowly up the entrance road. This had not been unexpected, but the timing was a little surprising. They thought it would be at least the next day before Martinez's men came to investigate. Nevertheless, Brian and Gracie quickly repeated their shut-down procedures and waited. Deluca's search was restricted to a quick visit to the command post and a fleeting glance through the dirty windows. It must have been obvious to Deluca that De Sousa's men would have searched the buildings. So Deluca must have decided there was nothing further he could do there and it wasn't long before he left. Brian was watching the feed from the security camera on his laptop and as soon as Deluca's limo turned off the road leading to their building Brian and Gracie felt it was their opportunity to complete their celebrations.

The next day the police returned to remove all of the computer equipment from the command post. Another team, forensic personnel wearing white overalls and masks, then entered to carry out an in-depth search for evidence. Brian and Gracie could hear them walking up and down the stairs, then carrying stuff out to their vehicles. During this time Brian and Gracie had to remain silent and motionless. They could hear the sounds from next door, so it was obvious the visitors in the command post would be able to hear them too if they were to move around. To relieve the tension Brian and Gracie pretended they were in a submarine as depicted in those old World War II movies where the slightest sound could be heard through the water. The problem was it took all their effort to prevent themselves from bursting into hysterical laughter. In addition, the use of the washroom was off limits and they were restricted to using their camping porta-potty which had been placed in the room furthest away from the command post wall. Their silence had to be maintained for a couple of more days, but once the forensic team left for the last time there were never any more visitors.

Brian had correctly calculated that the police would remove the computer equipment from the building for evidence-gathering. However, the police didn't have an inventory of the upstairs area so it wouldn't have occurred to them that appliances had been removed from the building. Even if they had obtained an inventory, they would just have assumed missing items had been stolen along with the truck and car. As for Martinez's people, none ever returned to the command post, except for Deluca's cursory search, and he had not gone upstairs so, they were none the wiser.

For the first few days of their isolation Brian and Gracie closely monitored the T.V. and radio reports of the theft on their computers and were pleased that all their acts of disinformation had been successful. For the next week Brian and Gracie lived in their temporary abode, taking turns to go outside for some sunlight and fresh air while the other monitored for visitors. Gracie took the opportunity to continue with her bird-watching; she could sit for hours with her binoculars studying the various water birds that frequented the river. At that time Gracie was envying the birds' freedom as they flittered from bush to tree, but she knew this arrangement for her was only temporary. However, she still could not get past the apprehension she was feeling about getting away with all this; but, then again, she wasn't as used to being a criminal as

Brian was. He was still laid-back and calm, as if everything they were doing was just fine.

When stuck inside the building they played games on their computers, made love, caught up with some reading and generally relaxed. Before they knew it, it was time for the next phase of the operation.

On the second Monday after the games Brian began to arrange appointments with managers of the ten leading banks in downtown Rio. His premise was that he represented a consortium taking care of the multitude of vendors that were plying their wares in the downtown core for the games. He explained that they had received very poor service from the bank they were currently with during the regular games and he was seeking a better service on behalf of the vendors to coincide with the opening of the para-games commencing the following week. However, he would provide more details at their meeting. These initial telephone conversations he carried out in almost perfect Portuguese. What appeared to have slipped through the cracks was that his mother, Maria, had been born in Lisbon and immigrated with her family to Canada at a very early age. Brian's father, David Beasley, was also an immigrant from Britain. He and Maria met, married, and after Brian was born, he was raised in a bilingual environment. The RCMP had not picked up on that when he was selected as a candidate for the undercover role, and Brian stuck with his stuttering Spanish to communicate with everyone in Brazil. Naturally Brian failed to mention it to anyone, as he felt there was always the possibility an opportunity might arise where his language skills would lead to a surprising advantage.

CHAPTER 34

The Con

Flávio Anderson strolled confidently into the office of Fernando Cortez, manager of a branch of one of the biggest banks in Brazil. Anderson was a tall slim man wearing a smart dark blue suit and carrying a black leather briefcase. He was handsome, with blonde hair and blue eyes, not quite the person Cortez had visualized during their telephone conversation when Anderson made the appointment. Cortez stood, looking solemn, as the visitor approached him and he held out his hand to receive a firm hand shake.

"Welcome Mr. Anderson," Cortez said, "please, sit down." Cortez was a young, serious-looking man slightly shorter than his visitor and a little overweight as a result of too many business lunches, indicated by the tight shirt that was fighting with its buttons to remain closed as Cortez sat down on his seat behind the desk.

"Good day Mr. Cortez, thank you for taking the time to meet with me," replied the man called Flávio Anderson as he sat down opposite Cortez.

"An unusual combination of names for this part of the world Mr. Anderson,." Cortez said stoically: it wasn't exactly a question, but Cortez was nonetheless seeking an answer in an attempt to feel out his prospective client.

"Yes," replied Anderson, laughing. "My father is originally from Sweden but he came to Rio as a teenager. He was playing for a lowly football club in Stockholm when he was spotted by a scout from the

Vasco Da Gama team. They brought him here, against my grandparents' wishes of course. He played a few games in the junior leagues but he wasn't deemed quite good enough to ever make the big club. The club was more than willing to pay for his return to Sweden but he had already met a girl so, he decided to stay, got married and here I am. As for Flávio –"

"Yellow hair." Cortez interrupted as Anderson pointed to his own blonde hirsute. They both laughed: the ice had been broken. Cortez continued. "Unfortunately Mr. Anderson, I am a Flamengo supporter. Is that a problem?" Anderson replied by feigning to leave as he learnt of Cortez's support for Da Gama's biggest rival, then they both laughed some more.

"Now, how can I help you Mr. Anderson?"

"Well, as I mentioned to you on the phone Mr. Cortez, a few months ago we set up a consortium to amalgamate most of the vendors that would be working the streets during the games," Anderson explained.

"Is there a name for your consortium Mr. Anderson?" Cortez asked.

"Oh sorry, forgot to mention that didn't I. The consortium's name is 'Rio's Raptors'. Contrary to the famous films they have been portrayed in, Raptors were actually flightless birds. As the poor of Rio have difficulty fleeing their plight we decided on that name," Anderson replied.

"Interesting play on words, Mr. Anderson," Cortez said smiling as he wrote down the name on a notepad.

"Not my suggestion I might add, but one of the ladies in the group suggested it," Anderson explained. "Anyway, the plan was to provide some of the unemployed people of Rio, those with limited skills, employment during the games so that they could benefit from some of the money that was heading for the coffers of corporate Brazil." Anderson paused for effect. The bank he was sitting in right now was indeed part of corporate Brazil and Cortez knew that as one of the sponsors his bank was profiting nicely from the deal. Anderson was appealing to the man's sense of charity. Anderson continued: "To facilitate this we would provide these people with all the pins, trinkets and game's merchandise to be sold to the public. You've seen them all over the city I am sure Mr. Cortez." Brian stopped and looked at Cortez for a response.

"Er, yes I have Mr. Anderson, and they all work for you?" Cortez asked. Naturally he had seen them. They were everywhere and, of course, the closer to the venues you got the more plentiful they were until as you arrived at the venues themselves, they virtually lined the streets.

"Well, not all of them. Unfortunately, as you know, there have been incidents where vendors have been a little too zealous to sell their wares. None of those incidents involved our people. We have rules and guidelines regarding the harassment of people but unfortunately all vendors are tarred with the same brush whether they are guilty or not. To minimize such incidents we would assign areas to vendors and provide them with routes. We strive to prevent confrontations with other vendors. In addition we would have people driving around the city to check on their welfare. In return, the vendors would return to warehouses in Rio to replenish their inventory with items they had sold that day. Their initial inventory we provided, then, using the income they had made, we would charge them for any new inventory plus a percentage of their initial portfolio. Remembering that the mark-up on these goods is high, so on a percentage basis their profit would be substantial. The expectation was that at some point during the games their initial inventory would be completely paid for and everyone would be making a profit by the end of the closing ceremonies."

"That's a wonderful concept Mr. Anderson," Cortez said, "and is it working out for everyone?"

"Yes and no," Anderson replied cryptically. "Yes, the vendors have worked very hard and our income has exceeded all of our expectations. Our overheads have been kept to a minimum and we are returning as much money back to the vendors as we possibly can."

"Well that's terrific isn't it?" Cortez asked.

"Yes it is, but sadly, we believe the bank we have been dealing with has short-changed us." Anderson said grimly. "Of course, we are dealing with cash and we can't prove a thing. You see, to reduce our costs we were hoping to rely on the bank to total our takes using their electronic bill counting machines that all banks have; otherwise we would have to employ people to count the money and make the necessary reports. Naturally, we thought they would be unnecessary overheads which would affect our bottom line, especially when the bank already had the staff and equipment to do the job. We would just be duplicating the effort. We were hoping the bank would provide us with the figures and we could return the profits to the vendors in the form of a dividend at the end of the games. We would also use some of the funds to invest in other programs to assist them beyond the games. Again, we were hoping the bank could provide us with expertise to maximize our returns." Brian paused and held out his arms. "I fear the operators of those machines at the bank were, how do you say, 'creaming off the top'."

"Really? That's terrible," Cortez said with genuine horror.

"Yes, I'm afraid so. We actually set a trap to prove our suspicions. One day we totaled up the cash and placed it in the bag in the usual way. We had double-checked the amount and we had even itemized the denominations so we had a total breakdown of the tally. Needless to say the deposit fell far short of the amount we had documented." Anderson paused shaking his head sadly.

"Did you contest it with the bank?" Cortez asked, absolutely astonished by these allegations.

"Indeed we did, but their response was that with the amount of cash coming into the branch it was inevitable that errors would be made and unless we could provide them with the totals up front they would not be in a position to accurately reconcile," Anderson responded.

"May I ask the name of the bank you were dealing with?" Cortez asked.

"I'd rather not say," Anderson replied, "I am aware of the serious allegations I am making and if it was to get back to the bank concerned our consortium may be at risk."

"I can assure you our conversation is in total confidence Mr. Anderson, but I understand your concern," Cortez said, "please continue."

"Of course, between the people from the security company delivering the money and the people at the bank I believe everyone knew when the money was being transferred and just about all the personnel were assisting in the money counting - hence the thefts. There was no client privacy and subsequently everyone knew. I think the word had been spread that we were representing just common street vendors and nobody cared. It's very disappointing. We are trying to provide a worthwhile service here, yet the recipients are being fleeced by their own people. We have already changed the security company we were dealing with and now we would like to change banks." Brian was beginning to sound passionate and his voice was quite emotional.

"I couldn't agree more, Mr. Anderson, and I can assure you that the type of behavior demonstrated by your current bank would not be tolerated at this bank. If you were to bring your business to us I would personally ensure only a skeleton staff would be aware of the delivery of the cash and we would provide you with an accurate reflection of the total amount received. We at this bank are totally committed to secrecy and client privacy. Furthermore, Mr. Anderson, I would be happy to provide you with an interest rate one point above the normal customer rate, because of the great work I believe you are doing," Cortez said, stressing his commitment by drumming his forefinger onto the desk.

"Really Mr. Cortez?" Anderson said sheepishly, "I don't know quite what to say."

"Say you will bring your business to us and we can get the paperwork rolling." Cortez said as he stood up and held out his hand for the shake that would seal the deal.

Of course Flávio Anderson, alias Brian Beasley, complied. Brian handed over a sizeable chunk of cash from his brief case as a deposit in the new account, nicknamed 'Rio's Raptors' and a postal address that was directed to a post office box. The necessary paperwork was signed and Brian was on his way to his appointment with the next mark. When he said a lady in the group suggested the name, it was indeed a partially true statement. Brian had suggested 'Raptors and Gracie had put forward 'Rio's Raptors', Brian had liked it and adopted it. Cortez fell for the whole spiel. Just as with the managers of the other banks Mr. Anderson had met with during the following few days, he had fed them a line and they were all taken: hook, line and sinker.

CHAPTER 35

Arranging Transport

In preparation for the meetings with the bank managers Brian had taken his suit to the dry cleaners, mainly for pressing; it was the same suit he had worn when they had arrived in Rio. He had ridden his bike to the nearest small town to the building they were holed up in. While he was in town he purchased bottles of hair dye, one of which he used to color his hair blonde in preparation for his scheduled meetings. The blue contact lenses had been procured by Gracie before coming to Brazil, together with some fake passports, driving licenses and other documentation Brian felt they might need. The contact lenses and some passports had been kindly supplied by the RCMP. All of this was concealed in the bottom of the carry-on luggage they had used for their trip to Brazil. But Brian had also arranged for a supply of extra fake passports through a dubious contact he had met during his incarceration and paid for from his illicit proceeds obtained during his first embezzlement. The briefcase he already had, so there was little else to supply for the disguise except a little bravado.

To travel to downtown Rio on the day of the scheduled meetings, Brian would cycle the few miles to the nearest train station, park and lock up his bicycle, then ride the train to Rio. In Rio he sought out a food court and used the washrooms to make his switch from cyclist to businessman. Brian wore a backpack which he opened to reveal his briefcase that contained his business uniform, consisting of his neatly folded suit, shirt and tie together with his dress shoes. He set the clothes out in the restricted space of the stall then stripped off his t-shirt, shorts and sneakers. He then dressed into the business clothes and placed his cycling garb in the briefcase, together with the backpack. He then placed the wads of money into the backpack so that none of the bank managers would be able to see the other money he was bringing for the other bank managers he would be meeting with that day. Brian emerged from the stall and checked himself in the mirrors over the sink, brushed his hair and left the food court to hail a taxi to his first appointment.

After all of his meetings for the day he would return to the same food court and change back into his cycling gear and return back to the 'pits'. This of course was all funded by the money taken from the ATMs that had been used for testing and training in the command post.

Meanwhile, Gracie began to work on two of the BOPE police uniforms that they had purloined on game day. She removed all references to 'police' and replaced them with the word 'security'. She removed the police emblems, embroidered new ones and sewed them back onto the uniforms. The uniform that Brian had worn on game day fitted him almost perfectly, but the smallest one available for Gracie needed to be taken in to provide her with a decent fit. Once Gracie had finished her alterations she tried on her new garb. Brian thought she looked quite sexy in those tight fitting trousers. The helmets still referred to the BOPE team, but changing those would have to wait a few days until Brian purchased some spray paint. But for the uniforms themselves Gracie was quite proud of her handiwork and they both looked rather spiffy in their black security suits with 'Delta Security' emblazoned on their uniform backs and badges.

A few days after the last meeting with the bank managers Brian again rode his bicycle into town. This time the purpose was to purchase a van that would suit their needs. They had found a suitable vehicle on one of the many web sites selling used cars. It was in the local area so Brian had phoned a couple of days ahead to ensure the availability of the black van and to confirm that cash payment would be agreeable. The used-car salesman stated they had no problem being paid in cash: they were not exactly a dealership for a major car company. The salesman then provided registration details of the van for Brian to contact his insurance company.

Two days later Brian arrived at the car lot and explained to a salesman who he was and that he had discussed the availability of a black van over the telephone a couple of days previously. It was actually the same salesman and once all the paperwork was completed and the money changed hands Brian loaded his bicycle into the back of the van and drove off the lot. Brian had showed the salesman conducting the sale a copy of his car insurance policy that he had downloaded. Brian had changed pertinent details such as his name and address; the car details which he had previously obtained from the salesman over the phone. The bogus policy was then printed in preparation for the purchase. Needless to say, the smooth talking Brian won over another victim.

Brian then drove to a hardware store where he purchased cans of spray paint, masking tape and Bristol board. His next stop was a medical equipment store where he purchased twenty laundry baskets, the type that are used in hospitals for soiled bed linen. These were large trolleys which when empty, could be pushed down, much like a baby buggy, to save space for transporting. The salesman at the store was a little suspicious and began to question why Brian needed so many baskets. But Brian had an answer for that. He explained to the gentleman that he was employed by a cleaning company working at the athletes' villages for the duration of the games. "Well you know what those athletes got up to during the party after the closing ceremonies?" Brian said and smiled lewdly. "Well the linen baskets seemed to be a popular place – whether the sheets were clean or not." Then they both smiled and Brian added, "well they weren't clean afterwards." They both laughed some more. "Judging by the way one of the trolleys had its sides bent I think there must have been a Russian shot putter in one of the baskets with a German weight lifter." By now the guy at the store couldn't stop laughing, so Brian thought that would be a good time to leave; the man even helped him load the baskets into the van, still smiling.

Before returning home Brian drove to a supermarket to purchase some groceries including fresh meat, sea food, fruit and vegetables. While he was in the supermarket he also picked up a few of the free newspapers that advertised classifieds and homes for sale in the area. Gracie had been monitoring the security feed and as soon as she saw the black van approaching with headlights flashing she had the doors wide open so Brian was able to drive right into the building while she closed the doors behind him. For the rest of the day they relaxed, then cooked a delightful meal of surf and turf followed by fresh-cut fruit and yogurt.

The following morning, after a breakfast of juice, cereal and coffee, Brian and Gracie got to work. They needed to put the logo on the van that would reflect the security company they were going to use to transport the money to the banks. They gathered all their tools and equipment and got to work. Gracie began to shape stencils from the Bristol board while Brian taped pages of the newspapers onto the side of the van with masking tape to shield it when spraying began on the logo. Once Gracie had finished her cutting they firmly taped the boards onto the side of the van and Brian did some tweaking with the newspaper and masking tape to ensure none of the van's side, other than around the Bristol boards, was exposed. Brian then picked up a can of white spray paint and violently shook it before aiming and spraying liberal amounts of paint into the cut out pieces of the boards. While the paint was drying on the van Brian picked up a can of black spray paint and gave it a good shake. Then he proceeded to spray the police helmets providing an all-round even coat until no reference of 'BOPE' could be seen. They then had a quick cup of coffee before gently removing the newspaper and boards from the van. They stood back to see a wonderful logo and the words 'Delta Security' neatly emblazoned in white on the side of the van. The logo and fonts were a perfect match to those Gracie had embroidered on the police BOPE uniforms and also identical to the letter-heading on the documentation they would provide to the bank for receipt of their laundry bags of money.

CHAPTER 36

Cash Delivery

The next day was the beginning of the para-games so Brian began to phone some of the banks he had contacted to inform them of the timing of their first deliveries. Brian and Gracie spent the remainder of the day filling five of the laundry trolleys with money and storing them in the van. The very next morning, at the crack of dawn, they drove into Rio, dressed in their security uniforms and helmets. They arrived at the first bank dead on time and it just happened to be the bank of Mr. Cortez. True to his word he was personally there to greet the security van at the rear of the bank. Brian climbed down from the cab and, with the helmet of his visor down, he emphasized his look around, for effect, to ensure it was safe to open the side door. He banged on the side of the van with his night stick and Gracie, also visor down, opened the door and jumped out. Between them they lifted out one of the laundry trolleys, then shut and locked the van door. Gracie walked the trolley to the rear of the bank while Brian professionally brought up the rear, constantly looking around for suspicious characters. Once they were inside the building and the door was secured Brian produced a clipboard bearing a document with the Delta Security logo at the top. The document outlined what the recipient was signing for as well as places for signatures for both the representative from the bank and from Delta Security. Brian signed both a top copy and the one underneath and indicated to Mr. Cortez to sign in the appropriate places on the form. Up until this point Brian had not needed to say anything, but now he had to mention to Mr. Cortez that they would be picking up the trolley the next time they were delivering there. Brian disguised his voice somewhat but between the helmet and the echoing walls of the bank's rear entrance there could have been no possible recognition from their previous meeting. Brian and Gracie had scheduled to make four more trips that morning and by just after lunch they were back at the 'pits'.

They spent most of the afternoon filling five more trolleys and loading them onto the van in preparation for deliveries the next morning to five other different banks. Brian made the phone calls to the banks for them to expect deliveries and then they began to prepare dinner. After dinner Brian was on his computer transferring a portion of the money they had deposited that day to another bank. Although the bank he was using had a Brazilian name it was 100% owned by a Swiss bank. Brian and Gracie owned a number of accounts with this bank, all under different names, of course. Once money was successfully deposited into these accounts, it was immediately transferred to US$ accounts in the Swiss bank's head office in Zurich. Due to Brazilian law, there were limitations as to how many Brazilian REALs could be converted to foreign currency. To avoid any unwanted attention, Brian ensured that these limits were not breached. At the bank in Zurich there was a standing order that stated once the target accounts hit US$ 10,000,000.00 they would withdraw the funds and arrange for a certain security company to collect the money. The security company had instructions to make the delivery to another bank in Zurich, where it was deposited into a numbered bank account. That is where the trail ended. The issuing Swiss bank had no idea of the destination bank; only the security firm would know that. The security company had no idea of what was being transported as for insurance purposes, all they needed to know was the value. So they had no inkling of what was being delivered to the other Swiss bank and, of course, because the destination was a numbered account the recipient bank didn't know what anyone was talking about.

This routine continued for another few weeks, long after the games were finished. Finally when all the money from four of the pits was depleted and it was time for Brian and Gracie to prepare to leave the country. There were still a few tasks that had to be accomplished before they left, one of which was to use black spray paint to remove any evidence of Delta Security, as they would be using the van to drive to the airport and leaving it in the long-term car park. They weren't sure what to do with the bikes. They could leave them upstairs, dump them in the river or take them in the van. In the end they decided to put them in the van, wipe them down to eradicate any fingerprints and leave them at the airport. Finally, Brian wanted to place 100 REAL notes in the pits in accordance with the number of the pit: it appealed to his sense of humor.

For their last supper they had a modest dinner using what rations that remained in the fridge. There was no point buying any more provisions. With everything completed, all they needed to do was get a good night's sleep, wake up and have breakfast before taking their time driving to the airport for an evening flight to Lisbon, Portugal.

CHAPTER 37

Heading Out

The next day they showered and dressed in the casual designer clothes they had purchased during their trips to Rio. Some days, after all their deliveries were complete, they would park the van in an underground car park to avoid suspicion. In the back of the van they would change out of their 'Delta Security' garb into t-shirts and shorts then go shopping. By now they had both dyed their hair black to coincide with the descriptions on the false passports they would be using when they eventually left the country. Before they left the 'pits' for the last time they fitted their contact lenses that provided them with what would be classified as dark brown eyes, which coincidently is what the descriptions were on their passport. After a quick look around to ensure there was no real incriminating evidence remaining in the building, Gracie opened the garage door and Brian drove the van through the entrance. Gracie brought their two bags of carry-on luggage and placed them in the back of the van before returning to the building to close the door. Gracie then climbed into the passenger seat and Brian dove the van to the long term car park of the main international airport in Rio, the very same airport they had arrived at all those months ago. They approached the terminal entrance as the recently married Mr. and Mrs. Costa travelling on their honeymoon to Lisbon.

At the terminal Brian had three large parcels that he arranged to be couriered to Filipe, José and Osvaldo. The parcels each contained a third of the remainder of the money from the command post's ATMs, less the expenses Brian and Gracie had incurred. This was still a substantial amount even after all their cash purchases. The van, plane tickets, food and sundries had all been paid for by cash. Not to mention a copious amount of cash they had converted to EUROs and US$ during their daily visits into town that they now had distributed around their persons. At first, Brian had been reluctant to send the parcel to José because he had suspected him of being the mole in the group and because José might report it to Martinez. If he did report it to Martinez, it would put Filipe's and Osvaldo's lives in jeopardy if they didn't report it back to Martinez. So Brian printed a little unsigned note for each of them that said:

<name>,

Thank you for all your assistance. I could have not done what I did without your help. But you are the only one of the team receiving a gift so it would be best if you told nobody about it. This is what was left from our testing.

Good Luck for the future - because you know we only have this many days remaining.

Of course, Brian was not aware of José's demise and because of the necessity for his untimely death Martinez was not supporting José's family. As a result, the receipt of a whole wad of money was extremely well received and would be enough to keep José's wife and children comfortable for the rest of their lives.

Brian and Gracie used the automated machines in the terminal to check in with the airline to receive their boarding passes. They were only each taking a carry-on and had no other luggage to check in. As they approached security with their first class return tickets and boarding passes Gracie began to show signs of increasing nervousness.

"Don't worry baby," Brian tried to calm her, "you were fine when we flew in from Canada."

"Yes, but I was undercover." Gracie replied, "if I get caught this time I'm going to end up in a Brazilian jail with no hope of extradition."

"It won't come to that," Brian replied, trying to console her. "Say nothing, leave all the talking to me and we'll be fine."

"Easy for you to say; you're already a criminal and you have nothing to lose." Gracie fired the barb that hit home. Brian stopped and faced her.

"Look, if you don't want to come, fine. Stay here. You'll end up in a Brazilian jail anyway, that's if Martinez doesn't get his hands on you first." Brian said with some anger, stressing the last point and the thought went through Gracie's mind, both figuratively and literally. "Remember, there's not much difference between you and me now. We are both criminals, except I am a habitual one." Brian said with a smile and he gave Gracie a hug and a kiss on her forehead. "Now come on, we'll be just fine."

There was a wicket available for first class ticket holders that was clear of passengers so they walked straight to the front and into the terminal proper. They withdrew their laptops and all electrical devices from their carry-ons and placed them into plastic trays for inspection. Brian then added his two wallets and loose change into his tray and Gracie placed her handbag into hers. They placed the plastic trays on to the conveyor belt that would pass the contents through the security x-ray machine for inspection. They then hoisted their carry-on bags onto the belt and proceeded to walk through the screening frame. There were no alarms triggered and no flags were raised with either their persons or the contents of their belongings. Brian and Gracie walked confidently in a bee-line for the executive lounge to receive a nerve-calming drink and some food.

Their flight was uneventful and with the help of a little wine Gracie slept soundly for most of the flight; but as soon as they disembarked the plane in Lisbon and headed for the immigration checks, her anxiety returned. Fortunately, because most of the passengers from their flight were still waiting at the baggage carousel, the line moved quickly so there wasn't much time for Gracie to dwell on her anxiety. They approached the immigration officer who was a stern-looking gentleman in his later years. He glanced briefly at both of them as he took their Brazilian passports and declarations of goods form that they had completed during the flight.

"Purpose of your visit to Portugal?" The immigration officer asked without looking up from the documentation he was reviewing."

"Vacation," Brian promptly replied, "honeymoon actually." Brian added and looked dreamily at a very uncomfortable Gracie trying to encourage her to smile. The immigration officer looked up at that statement and again glanced briefly at the pair of them.

"How long will your stay be here in Portugal?" The man said as he continued to look down at their documentation.

"We have a return flight in two weeks' time." Brian replied, a little concerned regarding the number of questions being asked and the attitude of the guy.

"Where will you be staying while you are here?" The man continued as though he was a call-center operator reading through a script.

"We will be staying for a couple of nights in Hotel Casablanca and then with relatives just outside Lisbon." Brian replied.

"Relatives?" The man asked and looked directly at Brian. But this time Brian was on safe ground having visited Lisbon many times to see his aunts and grandparents. Brian rattled off places, streets and names that seemed to placate the stern officer. The officer was just about to return the passports to Brian when he held them back and turned his attention to Gracie.

"You look a little worried," the immigration officer said as he paused to look at Gracie's passport for her name, "Maria, a little concerned regarding your visit to Lisbon?" Brian began to answer for her but the man interrupted him brusquely.

"Let the lady answer please." After a couple of seconds that seemed like an eternity to Brian, Gracie replied.

"I don't like planes." Gracie's reply was in very good Portuguese. Finally, something that moved the immigration officer; he gave a little 'hmph' and said, "you might be surprised to learn how few people do my dear," then he returned the passports to Brian. Brian and Gracie grabbed their luggage and walked through immigration and into the terminal. They would not have to worry about borders and immigration for some considerable time.

Gracie was almost physically sick with nerves after their encounter with immigration, but Brian was merely smiling with that 'see I told you so' grin, as if there was nothing that could have possibly gone wrong. They had rehearsed a few Portuguese phrases and when to say them which would be prompted by Brian using varying body language. The 'plane' phrase was indicated by Brian looking upwards to the ceiling and

Gracie responded perfectly. Between her nervous state and explanation it was certainly enough to convince the wizened, experienced immigration officer. She was a fast learner.

Brian and Gracie could now relax and act like regular American tourists, just as their passports and accompanying documentation stated: Mr. and Mrs. Donovan. After their self-imposed imprisonment in the 'pits' it was just a thrill to enjoy their freedom and eat some delicious meals. Not to mention the purchase of the finest clothes that Emma Donovan was now enjoying at Jason Donovan's expense. However, the main reason to remain in Lisbon for a few days was to await the receipt of their banking credentials from Brian's bank in Zurich. Brian had called the bank manager on arrival at their hotel in Lisbon, prompting the manager to send credit cards, banking cards and cheque books by express courier. When the documentation arrived they now had their financial independence, so they immediately went to the Porsche dealership and purchased the latest Carrera model from the shop floor. Of course the salesman was reluctant to sell because it would be a few days, maybe weeks, before he could replace the model and until then he would have nothing to display. But Brian overcame all the salesman's objections and the next day Mr. and Mrs. Jason Donovan began their road trip to Zurich.

Brian estimated that they would need five days of driving to reach Zurich; however the route they had chosen included Madrid, Barcelona, Andorra and Montpellier. Naturally, they were now extremely rich tourists so they could spend as much time as they liked sight-seeing and enjoying some of the local culinary specialties. There was much to do and see in both Madrid and Barcelona. Gracie was particularly enthralled by the art museums in the two cities containing early Picasso and other painters of the period. In Barcelona they both enjoyed the antics of the street performers on La Rambla as well as beholding the contents of its endless shops and bars. In the evening they tasted the local dishes of gazpacho and paella and imbibed a few pitchers of sangria. The visit to Andorra necessitated a spectacular drive up into the Pyrenees and there was some early snow on some of the mountain peaks. The first snow they had seen since leaving Canada.

By the time they arrived in Zurich, all the money had been safely ensconced in their numbered account, so all Brian would need to do was finalize some banking transactions and to close their interim accounts with the bank that had been receiving the funds from Rio de Janeiro. By now their hair had almost all returned to their natural colors and once they had got used to saying their new names they wouldn't have to pretend anymore.

It was now late Thursday afternoon in Zurich, so Brian decided it was too late to contact his bank; he would telephone them in the morning. They decided that with all the travelling they had been doing they would just relax in their hotel room that evening, have a couple of drinks and select some meals from the room-service menu. The next morning Brian contacted his bank manager and he agreed to accommodate him at 10:00 AM, so by midday all Brian's banking dealings were complete. Brian and Gracie celebrated that evening a little too heavily and the next morning it took them a few hours to recover before deciding what they were going to do next. Gracie had never been to Europe before and Brian's previous visits had been restricted to travelling to Portugal to visit his mother's extended family. His father had never shown any interest in visiting his home country of England as he had very few relatives left alive.

Ultimately, they would need a place to live and it was obvious it was going to be in one of the European Mediterranean countries. They felt the best thing to do was spend a couple of months driving around Europe to come up with a couple of potential locations: after all, money was no object. First they would drive down the west coast of Italy, take in Florence and Rome before circling up the east coast to Venice. On the way they could enjoy the many towns on the Adriatic as well as San Marino and Rimini. Just the sound of these places was enough to get Gracie excited and she couldn't wait.

The route agreed, their first stop would be Milan, where they would spend a couple of days before driving on to Pisa to witness the leaning tower for themselves. But that was not for another couple of days. Before they departed, Brian wanted to call Martinez. He put the cell phone that Martinez had given him on charge. He hadn't used it since the day of the heist and he wasn't even sure that the number in the contact list was still valid. While it was on charge Brian and Gracie went shopping and to have a coffee at a nearby bistro. Gracie was really excited to visit Italy, especially Florence, a city steeped in art and history. On their return to the hotel they quickly showered and changed in preparation for a dinner party hosted by Brian's bank manager. They were enjoying a cocktail in their hotel room when Brian unplugged the phone from its charging cable and made the call to Martinez.

Beasley put his phone on speaker so that Gracie could listen in on the dialogue between Martinez and Beasley. Gracie had been a little nervous about making the call; she thought it was unnecessary, but Brian felt it was only fair that Martinez received some of the money. After all, it might get him off their back.

"You could have written or sent him an email to tell him where it is." Gracie suggested.

"That would have left a paper trail and anyway, where's the fun in that?" Beasley replied.

CHAPTER 38

Touring

Brian and Gracie spent one more day in Zurich before heading for Milan. In Milan they spent a couple of days before visiting the historic town of Pisa. However, once they had visited the tower and walked around Pisa it was a case of 'been there, done that' and Gracie was eager to continue on their journey inland to Florence. The next morning after breakfast they packed their overnight bags and Gracie went to the car while Brian proceeded to the foyer to check out. There was a small problem with the bill that delayed the payment procedures. At first Brian felt some trepidation as he thought it was a problem with his card or his identity but it turned out to be an unfortunate clerical error caused by the overnight hotel staff, for which the hotel manager apologized profusely. Brian waved the problem off and everyone was all smiles as Brian turned to exit through the ornate glass doors of the hotel. Brian's smile instantly disappeared. Standing there, flanked by two Italian Carabinieri was Lieutenant-colonel Manuel De Sousa and Detective Sergeant Dexter Davis.

"Going somewhere Brian?" Davis asked.

"Surprised to see an old fart like me here?" De Sousa asked. Brian was lost for words: he had no idea how they could have possibly found him there. Davis didn't look well but De Sousa was positively beaming after finally catching up with Beasley.

"We've had someone following you since Zurich, Brian," Davis offered, but was obviously in some discomfort as he spoke and stared at the still stunned look on Brian's face. "But from past experiences we thought it might be a little easier to extradite you from Italy rather than Switzerland. So here we are. Please to see us are you?" Brian could not have been more devastated. The blood had drained from his face and he felt numb. It was the worst feeling he had ever felt in his life. But if he thought that was bad, as De Sousa and Davis parted to let him through and one of the carabinieri came forward to clap him in wrist restraints he saw something else that shook his very being. Parked outside the hotel where his Porsche was supposed to be was a shiny black limo. The driver's window was down and staring at him with an evil sneer was the big brute of a man that was Deluca's driver and henchman. Beside him, standing casually against the car, cross-legged with arms crossed across his chest was a relaxed Deluca, wearing the mandatory sunglasses. Deluca was smiling at him and as Brian's gaze drifted to the back of the car he could see seated in the rear seat, her shoulders heaving with sobs, a very terrified Gracie.

Epilogue

It had been a few weeks since Brian and Gracie were apprehended in Italy and De Sousa had been invited to a Halloween party hosted by Diego Martinez. In addition to being a party, it was also a benefit function for a new charity Martinez had created. De Sousa and Martinez had kept in close communication during the build-up to the arrest of both Beasley and Brown. During this period De Sousa had reiterated the scam Beasley had pulled for the banks to accept his cash deposits. Although it was a complete con, Martinez had thought the actual premise was not a bad idea. Consequently, Martinez contacted a few of his legitimate businesses to assign staff to form a consortium to provide some portable selling booths for some of the poor of Rio de Janeiro. They would populate high-traffic tourist areas and, identical to Beasley's mythical vendors, they would be provided with their initial inventory and they would eventually return to purchase more with money received. They would also receive benefits, disability and medical benefits and the possibility of a real job in one of Martinez's many organizations. The consortium was yet to be named but Martinez had received high praise from the authorities and they fully supported the charitable approach Martinez was offering.

A number of government high rollers were in attendance so that Martinez could feather his nest, together with the usual smattering of politicians, celebrities and rich friends to begin to fill the coffers of the consortium. The invitations suggested fancy dress but it wasn't mandatory; prizes would be awarded but it wasn't a competition, Martinez would just pass out prizes because he could. Later in the evening Martinez would also announce a competition to provide a name for his new consortium, together with a nice prize for the person who selected the winning moniker.

Most people chose to wear elaborate costumes, but Martinez himself chose to dress as Zorro, with an eye-mask which did nothing to provide him with any disguise. The rest of his costume was simply black clothes and a cape, but no hat. De Sousa, ever the conservative, just arrived in casual shirt, slacks and blazer. He told anyone who asked that he was dressed as a retiree, which is exactly what he was.

The party was in full swing when Martinez caught De Sousa's attention and indicated that they should meet down in the office. Martinez walked inconspicuously down the spiral staircase situated in the main ball room while De Sousa exited the room and walked down the stairs by the front door. Martinez was already seated, with his mask off, when De Sousa entered the room.

"Manuel, congratulations on your retirement. Was it a sudden decision?" Martinez asked.

"Thank you Diego. Sudden decision? Not really," De Sousa replied. "After Beasley was apprehended the powers that be held an inquiry and deemed that I was not responsible for how events unfolded. My record would remain unblemished, with the caveat that I announce my retirement, in which case I would receive a full pension. The official line is that I decided to take the opportunity to retire. To be honest Diego, I would have gone even if they hadn't asked me to. I'd had enough," De Sousa said with finality. "I gave my life to the force Diego, you know that." Martinez nodded his head in agreement while De Sousa added. "All those years and now, well it's just not worth thinking about."

"I'm sorry my friend I truly am," Martinez said, and he meant it. "I feel I am partially responsible for how things have turned out and if there is anything I can do for you Manuel, you know that."

"I appreciate that Diego, but then it would be seen as I truly am in bed with the enemy," De Sousa replied.

"Not so, Manuel and I'll tell you why presently and anyway, I own legitimate businesses. Personnel at these businesses attend seminars and I could easily arrange for you to be a guest speaker. It pays handsomely: best hotels, finest foods. No connection to me could be traced, invitations would arrive from legitimate agencies and you could do what you have always dreamed of doing. Once your reputation grows, who knows? International conventions, TV interviews. Give it some serious thought, Manuel. As you say, you don't owe your ex-employers anything, the way they have treated you. You are the most honest cop I have ever known," Martinez said, and again, it was sincerely intended.

"High praise indeed Diego, I thank you for that," De Sousa replied humbly. Diego sat back and waited for De Sousa to continue but his next topic of conversation was not what he expected.

"One thing that I have not been able to ascertain Diego. How did you know where Beasley and the girl were?" De Sousa asked. There was a pause while Martinez considered answering the question but he trusted De Sousa, so he decided to tell him.

"Simple. The phone," Martinez said proudly.

"Phone, what phone?" De Sousa asked.

"I give certain operatives 'pay as you go' phones that are untraceable. Each one has a number in their built-in contact list that they can call to reach me in the event of an emergency and vice versa. The number that is called is another untraceable phone that is answered by my communications guys here in the building. In some cases, such as Beasley, there is a phone dedicated to only them. Consequently, when that phone rings we know exactly who is calling." Martinez explained.

"But that doesn't explain how you knew where he was when he called you that night." De Sousa said.

"Well, Beasley is not the only one with computer skills Manuel. One of our men in the communications room wrote an app. The app. is hidden on all the phones that we give to the operatives. When an outgoing call is made, the app. will determine the location by using its built-in GPS. It will then send a text to the phone that is dedicated to the caller in question with the caller's location and also the latitude and longitude co-ordinates. The text would be deleted from the sender's phone so the caller would never know it has been sent. Consequently, when that call was made from Beasley, I handed the phone back to Eduardo and we drove to the 'pits'. If you remember, that was where I received a call. It was the communications guy telling me Beasley was staying at a hotel in Zurich."

"That simple," De Sousa said amazed.

"That simple," Martinez agreed with a smile before continuing. "I arranged for a private investigator to keep tabs on them before I decided what to do about them." At this De Sousa balked and looked a little hurt.

"So you didn't tell me straight away? Were you thinking of keeping it from me?" De Sousa asked, not a little miffed by the revelation.

"Now take it easy Manuel. I was going to tell you - of course I was. I even alluded to it after I finished the call, if you remember. No, I simply wanted my money back and I needed some time to think how I could obtain the information from Beasley," Martinez said in a calm voice, trying to placate De Sousa. "But by the time we had counted all the money from the pits and I decided I had at least covered my expenses plus more, so I was ahead of the game. That's when I felt the time was right to inform you." There was a pause in the conversation. Then Martinez added, "I am still hoping we can persuade Gracie to share the Swiss bank account number with us." At the sound of Gracie's name De Sousa perked up noticeably.

"Gracie? How is she doing?" De Sousa asked with a concerned look on his face.

"Oh she's fine." Martinez replied with a smile. "She is helping Pedro with the grounds and I think she is actually enjoying it."

"I'm sure you have had discussions with her about her involvement in all this," De Sousa said.

"Yes of course I have," Martinez replied brusquely. "She claims she was completely under Beasley's spell. She think he may have drugged her somehow, but there is no proof to substantiate that. No, she was smitten and he manipulated her, he is one smooth bastard, I'll give him that. But she still claims she doesn't know the number of the bank account in Switzerland, but I think she is lying."

"How do you propose to obtain that information?" De Sousa asked.

"Oh I just think I will threaten to take her away from under Pedro's wing, who is a happily married family man, and let her, shall we say, work under some of the guards, unless of course she would like to share some information with us," Martinez said coolly. De Sousa squirmed a little at the thought of what those men were capable of doing to her, knowing some of the goons that Martinez had working for him. But he had another idea.

"Perhaps, I might suggest I take care of her and try and persuade her to tell us what we need to know. After all I am a retired police officer, one of her kind," De Sousa said meekly.

"You, Manuel, what would you do with her?" Martinez laughed somewhat surprised at the suggestion.

"I need a travelling companion, someone who could help me with my appointments and preparations, much like an Admin. Secretary," De Sousa replied.

"But how would you explain having a corrupt policewoman working for you? You have already told the authorities that you were unable to find her when you arrested Beasley. The plan was that once I was done with her I would hand her over to you. You would claim you had never ceased to search for Beasley's accomplice and you finally captured her," Martinez stated.

"I know. I know. But I'm not enamored with the way I have been treated by the authorities and now into my first few weeks of retirement I realize how desperately lonely I am and a companion could be what the doctor ordered. Besides, except for you and me, nobody in Brazil knows who she is," De Sousa said.

"But that RCMP guy knows who she is, and then there's her contact here in Rio," Martinez replied.

"Unfortunately, Dexter Davis has cancer. It doesn't look terminal but he will be undergoing treatment for quite some time. He will be placed on long-term disability and eventually retired from the RCMP. I'm certain the last thing he cares about is an unaccounted-for policewoman in Brazil. As for Debbie Tansley, her husband was posted back to the States, so all contact with her is gone. Of course, if Gracie decided to become a flight risk and attempt to leave the country then all bets are off. Eventually, I am sure we can arrange for her to set foot back in Canada without any consequences," De Sousa simply said.

"Well you old dog," Martinez let out. "O.K. let's play that out. If she does stay with you and shares the number of the account with you, what are you going to do with that information?" Martinez inquired.

"First, I will find out the balance of the account. Then I will discuss with you a reasonable share to be procured for your additional expenses; of course it would be untraceable. Then I will let the authorities know of the banking details and they can fight over what proportion of the money is returned to the Brazilian and Canadian banks." De Sousa sat back. The ball was now in Martinez's court.

"Hmm," Martinez mused. "Sounds fair. So you get Gracie, I get an extra bonus, which I will donate to my charity, the banks receive some money back and the police have closed the case."

"Win, win all ways round." De Sousa said.

"Except for Beasley." Martinez said.

"Except for Beasley." De Sousa agreed.

"On the subject of Beasley, what is happening with him?" Martinez asked.

"He is currently languishing in a prison in Italy. Canada has applied to Italy for extradition, but so has Brazil. How we think it is going to be played out is that, as an escaped felon, he will be returned to Canada to complete his sentence," De Sousa answered.

"Escaped felon! I thought they helped him escape," Martinez said.

"Who did?" De Sousa asked rhetorically. "There's no documentation to support that and the claims Beasley has made that there was a policewoman assisting him, a Miss Gracie Brown, are so far unsubstantiated. The last anyone knows is that Miss Brown quit the force and disappeared. There is no proof that she came to Brazil as Beasley tells us. He swears that she travelled with him under the pseudonym of Sandra Essex and she got married here. Unfortunately, we can't seem to trace any record of a marriage of Gracie Brown or even a Sandra Essex. It is definitely a shame that sometimes our record-keeping is not as good as it should be, tut tut tut. But I digress. Brazil will then have to request extradition from Canada which might take, oh I don't know, how long is Beasley's sentence in Canada? Ten years? So, extradition may take as much as nine years, then he will be sent to Brazil for trial."

"What about the statute of limitations?" Asked Martinez, "surely it would be applicable by then."

"Because he has already been charged and an extradition order applied for, the statute of limitations would not apply," De Sousa explained.

"But that brings up another problem. Beasley can still talk and once he finds out his money has all gone, he will chirp like a canary," Martinez said.

"What's he going to say?" De Sousa questioned. "The heist was an undercover operation, until he went rogue. His testimony is no longer credible. We interviewed the people who worked for him: Filipe and Osvaldo and the unfortunate third person, José, who is no longer with us. Osvaldo was just a cook and chief bottle washer. According to Osvaldo, he was hired by Beasley and the man knows nothing. As for Filipe, a computer techy, he thought he was working for someone who was developing ATM software that he would be selling to the banks. Filipe thought he was working on the ground floor of a technological breakthrough, something he would be able to cash in on – legally. He denies having any knowledge of illicit dealings and we can't prove that he did. Now, apparently Beasley told the RCMP that Filipe did a test-run for the heist at a bank across town. We interviewed the people who worked there, but none of them could identify Filipe as the man who had the problem with the ATM. Now, having said that, I'm not sure if they had taken the correct photograph for identification." De Sousa paused and looked at Martinez conspiratively, "although, I must confess I am somewhat confused as to how both Osvaldo and Filipe are now driving flashy, expensive cars. We asked them where they got the money from and they just said they had been saving up over the years." Martinez laughed at that. "You know something don't you Diego?" De Sousa questioned.

"Yes, I do." Martinez replied, still laughing. "Both Osvaldo and Filipe are very loyal, honest, trustworthy thieves. They each received a package from Beasley that was accompanied with a note basically telling them not to discuss the money with the others as they alone were receiving some compensation. Well, after a few days of deliberating whether they should tell each other, they got together and discussed whether they should come clean and tell me that they had received the money. Eventually, they arranged a meeting with me and told me that they had received some money by courier from Beasley. I'm assuming from what Filipe and Osvaldo alluded to that the proceeds came from the cash in the ATMs that were used for testing, not part of the take from the banks' ATMs. But by then we had located the money in the 'pits' so I just told them to keep it; they had earned it after all. I don't even know how much they received. I didn't ask. I'm assuming José's wife also received a third of the proceeds but I didn't pursue it. Let her keep it too," Martinez explained.

"At least Beasley showed some class then." De Sousa mumbled sarcastically.

"And we also have him to thank for this new chartable initiative for the poor of Rio," said Martinez. "I think it is a wonderful idea."

"And just how much will you make off this racket, Diego?" De Sousa asked. Martinez just lazily rolled his eyes and said,

"You cut me to the quick, Manuel. I assure you, this will be an honest charity, executed by legitimate businesses and all proceeds will be returned to the appropriate people of Rio."

"Define appropriate," Manuel asked.

"Seriously Manuel," Martinez said, "all I have done is initiated the charity. The day-to-day running of the consortium is out of my hands. I honestly believe this will do some good."

"O.K. O.K. Diego, I believe you." Manuel laughed.

"There's another thing, Manuel," Martinez said with all seriousness. "I touched on it earlier. You have been an inspiration to me, your tireless search for the truth and lifelong endeavor to fight crime. Because of that I have decided to wind down all of my illegal activities and just concentrate on my legitimate businesses, which, I might add, are extremely profitable." Martinez stopped talking to enjoy the total look of surprise on De Sousa's face. "That's right Manuel, you are now looking at an honest man and I have you to thank for that. I am still a very rich man, and I don't need to encourage young men to invest in a life of crime. Although I fear the vacuum I leave will be filled by my current competitors. The police will now have a devil they don't know which may be infinitely worse than 'Diabo Diego'." Martinez used his street name, the name Manuel had fought against his entire working life. "I guess you could take some solace in the fact that although you never successfully charged me with anything, you are solely responsible for the cessation of my life of crime."

"Wow, that's going to take time to sink in, the devil Diego an honest man!" Said De Sousa astonished. "What will happen to Deluca and that driver of his; and all the guards you have around here?"

"No change, Deluca will remain my right hand man, with his driver of course only now their dealings will all be above board." Martinez replied casually. "As for the guards, I will still require their services, there's a lot of criminals around I will need protection don't you know?" They both laughed.

"But what will you do with all your free time Diego?" De Sousa asked almost jokingly, "Crime requires planning and you have become a master at it. If you're not doing that anymore what will you do?"

"Ha, so true. Well, like yourself Manuel, I'm not as young as I once was and it has become a burden constantly coming up with sophisticated plots. But the most difficult part is to keep everything at arm's length, so if things do go tits-up nothing could ever be pinned on me," Martinez explained.

"The bank heist being a prime example," De Sousa said.

"Exactly. The bank heist is a great example," Martinez agreed and pointed to De Sousa to emphasize the point. "And anyway, with you retired who am I going to be up against? It won't be any fun anymore" At that they both laughed before Martinez continued. "No, Manuel I have decided to do some travelling. I have spent most of my adult life cooped up here in this mansion. It is time to fly the coop as it were. There's something else, I know I have a reputation for enjoying the company of pretty girls, I could hardly be referred to as a misogynist."

"No, that you can't Diego." De Sousa said with a licentious glint in his eye. Martinez smiled and continued his thought.

"But I have quite taken to a lady here. Before you say anything it's not what you think, she is actually the mother of one of the girls who came to work for me but the girl was far too young and her mother was not backward in coming forward to tell me so. She came chasing after me to take her daughter away and she gave me a piece of her mind. She is a single mother and subsequently very protective of her only child, I admired her courage and she has since become a regular visitor here. So we have decided we would like to travel together and you never know, we may settle down."

"Wow. That is some turnaround, she must be something special indeed." De Sousa remarked quite taken aback.

"She is. But you know what Manuel? All these celebrities and politicians attending this party are pleasant to my face but behind my back...." Martinez let the sentence trail off before continuing, "I know what they say and I am not immune to all the vitriol. I used to be when I was a stupid, young kid but now it's no longer necessary and I am ready for a change." When Martinez finished speaking De Sousa was lost for words and they were both feeling a little emotional which spawned a short lull in their conversation. When the silence was broken it was almost as a sidebar as Martinez asked De Sousa another question.

"Talking of the bank heist, that's another thing that bothers me Manuel. You and Beasley were working in cahoots together up until the time he drove off. Surely there would have to have been some incriminating evidence that could have been produced against me. You're not holding anything back are you?" Martinez said.

"Like what?" De Sousa replied. "Remember, there is absolutely no written documentation remaining. All those notes from Gracie that were delivered to me, and me alone, via Debbie no longer exist. As far as the authorities are concerned Gracie can't be found and Debbie is no longer here. The only person who could say anything is me, and now that I have retired my memory is nowhere near as good as it used to be." De Sousa paused; Martinez was smiling. "Anyway, everything Beasley did to steal all that money can be said he was doing for himself. What involvement did you have? You had one meeting with him. Nobody can prove what was said. We all thought he was working for us to obtain his freedom when all the time the little bastard saw it as an opportunity to make a big killing and take off. No Diego, I don't think there is a scrap of evidence that he can provide that points to you as the perpetrator of this scandalous crime. And anyway, do you honestly believe that the police forces and banks of this country would like to be dragged through the courts, admitting to an undercover setup where they lost US$ 500,000,000, only to pay out even more in interest when the thief deposited the money back into the banks? That's adding insult to injury.

No, I don't think so. Especially if we can recover some of their money. And now that you are on the straight and narrow, I can retire in peace." De Sousa said, smiled and sat back.

"But what about the extradition order? There would have to be some sort of trial surely?" Martinez asked.

"By then it would all be forgotten and the authorities would probably charge him with a misdemeanor or some trumped up charge, if at all. As I said earlier, I don't believe anyone want to drag this mess through the courts." De Sousa replied.

Neither spoke for a moment until Martinez called for Eduardo. Martinez moved his hulk of a frame forward and almost whispered to De Sousa.

"Manuel I am going to do something now that I have never done in my life. That is how much I appreciate what you have done for me and how I trust our little pact. I don't have many friends, I have many acquaintances, as you can see from the turnout of my parties, but very few real friends. Yet, you my arch enemy, I value as my best friend." Martinez said then turning to Eduardo. "Bring Manuel one of our finest Scotches – sorry Eduardo, make that two." When Eduardo returned he placed both glasses of whiskey in front of De Sousa. Martinez smiled and said to the butler, "no Eduardo, one of them is for me." Poor Eduardo was confused, and at first he just stood there like a deer in the headlights of a cat. Eduardo had worked for Martinez ever since the man had made his first million and had never known him to have any drink containing alcohol. Eduardo was astonished.

"For you sir?" Eduardo asked, but before Martinez could answer De Sousa had slid one of the glasses over to Martinez.

"Saude!" Said Martinez.

"Saude!" Echoed De Sousa. They both drank while the poor butler stood watching in bewilderment, then turned and left the room shaking his head.

"It's a great shame Manuel," said Martinez as the fiery liquid of fine scotch spread down his throat. "Beasley had a great criminal mind and he would have been a marvelous long term asset to my organization, if of course I had chosen to remain in that line of business. It's a great pity." They both thought about that for a minute as they slowly drank the remainder of their drinks.

They both returned to the party the way they had left and no one was any the wiser that they had disappeared together. Both men mingled with the guests but De Sousa noticed that Martinez spent most of the evening laughing and talking with a more mature but very attractive looking woman, obviously the new object of his affections. De Sousa had to admit, the couple looked very happy together. Towards the end of the evening Martinez had an opportunity to introduce De Sousa to his new girlfriend. De Sousa was very impressed with both her beauty and her demeanor, he could certainly see what Martinez saw in her. De Sousa was sure she would be good for his new best friend, she was quite the catch and said as much to the big man. In return, Martinez pointed to where Gracie was selecting some deserts from a table in the corner of the room. De Sousa thought she looked lonely, yet so beautiful and he walked casually over to her to say 'hi'. They began to chat at great length discussing his speaking engagements and the travelling that would result from them. Gracie appeared to be genuinely interested, then the subject changed to what she had been up to of late. Gracie told him she was being well taken care of at the mansion but she felt it would be nice to leave. However, because of her recent past, her options were somewhat limited and she wasn't sure what the future held for her. As a parting farewell just before De Sousa left the party he told her not to worry and assured her that everything was going to turn out for the best. During their conversation they had never discussed anything to do with the robbery or Beasley.

After breakfast the next morning Martinez phoned Gracie to inform her that she was leaving the mansion, she should pack and be prepared to leave in an hour. She was informed that Deluca and his driver would be taking her to her new home. That in itself was enough to cause her distress. However, Martinez gave her a few, friendly parting words that eased her anxiety a little.

"Have a nice life Gracie, I know you will."

Deluca and the omnipresent whale of a man he called his driver arrived outside De Sousa's modest home. Coincidentally, it was not a far cry from where Brian and Gracie had their apartment when they first arrived in Rio. Deluca had phoned ahead to De Sousa so the smiling, relaxed man was already waiting at his front door ready to greet his new guest. After the limo came to a halt both Deluca and the ogre that was his driver got out of the vehicle. Deluca opened the rear door of the limo and Gracie, still unaware of her fate, nervously exited from the rear of the car with her single carry-on bag.

THE END

Printed in the United States
By Bookmasters